The train was well into the mountains now, moving quite slowly.... All of a sudden most of the windows on the right hand side of the car blew inwards under a hail of gunfire.

"This is it!" Raider shouted.

A dozen men were running downslope through the pines, firing at the train as they came on. The train windows erupted in flashes of flame from at least a dozen gun muzzles, and a hail of lead flew their way.

Raider crawled along the floor, encouraging the defenders. Broken glass crunched under his knees. "Damn it, Duke!" he shouted. "Get your head outta that window! You're gonna be seein' things through an extra eye if you stick your head up that way."

Raider left him alone. He had other things to worry about. Like staying alive. Like dynamite. In a little while it would be dark enough for one of them to crawl close enough to lob a stick of dynamite under the car and blow it wide apart...

J. D. HARDIN

TRAIN RIDE TO HELL

BERKLEY BOOKS, NEW YORK

TRAIN RIDE TO HELL

A Berkley Book/published by arrangement with
the author

PRINTING HISTORY
Berkley edition/April 1987

ISBN: 0-425-09713-7

A BERKLEY BOOK ® TM 757,375
Berkley Books are published by The Berkley Publishing Group,
200 Madison Avenue, New York, N.Y. 10016.
The name "BERKLEY" and the stylized "B" with design are trademarks
belonging to Berkley Publishing Corporation.

PRINTED IN THE UNITED STATES OF AMERICA

CHAPTER ONE

"Goddamn it...I itch," Raider snarled, shrugging his shoulders and arms inside his heavy coat.

"Of course," Doc replied. "A wool coat? In New York? In June? If you hadn't insisted on bringing along that hogleg of yours, and that pigsticker you call a knife..."

Raider shrugged again. "Had to. Don't feel right without 'em. Hell, you should talk, you're packin' a pistol too."

"Of course. After all, we are supposed to be protecting the man. But it's a question of size, Raider. That cannon of yours..."

"It's a damn sight better'n that popgun you got," Raider muttered, jerking his chin in the direction of the slight bulge under Doc's light mohair and silk jacket, where he was carrying his Smith and Wesson break-top .32 in a shoulder holster. "Couldn't protect a squirrel with a toy like that. Hell...probably couldn't even *kill* a squirrel."

"At least I don't look like a refugee from a blizzard," Doc replied, sneering at Raider's coat. It was not only heavy, but it was long. With big pockets. Big enough to hold the heavy Remington .44 that Raider had stuffed into the right front pocket. He was also wearing his bowie knife on the left side of his belt. The protruding handle of the eighteen-inch weapon did little to help the cut of the coat.

"Don't see why I couldn't o' just worn the gunbelt," Raider mumbled.

"Raider, people just don't wander around a city like

1

New York hung with artillery. Well, they don't do it openly, anyway."

"Yeah, it sure is one damn sneaky place. Phony as hell. An' damned hot. Sticky, too," Raider grumbled, changing the subject. Doc nodded in agreement. It was only June, but the stifling, humid New York summer heat had settled in early.

The two of them were on foot, heading toward the waterfront. They formed a considerable contrast. Raider was tall, rawboned, saddle-hard, wearing jeans and a trail shirt under the overcoat. His boots were horseman's boots, high-heeled, scuffed and worn, but obviously handmade and of the finest quality. He'd left his gunbelt and his short black leather jacket in the hotel room, but still wore his battered black Stetson. Stalking along, black eyes scowling under the drooping brim of the Stetson, thick black mustache curling down around the sides of his mouth, he was clearly no city dweller.

Doc, on the other hand, was smaller and deceptively soft-looking. He was dressed in the latest city fashion: a well-cut silk and mohair suit with a vicuña vest, a silk shirt and cravat, Melton overgaiters, and highly polished button-up shoes. A neatly brushed and well-blocked pearl-gray derby covered his fair hair. He carried a silver-headed walking stick in his right hand, which he swung back and forth in rhythm to his stride rather than using it to lean on. However, despite his careless elegance, there was a slight sheen of sweat on his well-scrubbed face. He too was feeling the heat.

"I wonder how long we're gonna have to nursemaid this old coot?" Raider said. "Hell, when I signed on with the agency I never thought it'd come to this. I mean, whatta we call him, anyhow? Your Holy Worship? Your Dukeship?"

"He's a Grand Duke," Doc corrected. "Normally, you'd call a duke, 'Your Grace,' but Wilhelm is a grand duke, a ruler, so we call him, 'Your Highness.'"

"That don't set too well with me," Raider said sourly. "I don't figure anybody oughtta be set up higher'n anybody else." He grinned then. "Hell, maybe I'll just call him Willie."

"I'd really rather you didn't, Raider. I rather suspect Mr. Pinkerton would rather you didn't either."

Not for the first time, Doc wondered why he and Raider had been chosen for this particular assignment. To be more exact, he wondered why Raider had been chosen. Doc had little difficulty seeing how he himself fit into the picture. With his Harvard education and general background of culture and breeding, it was only natural that they'd selected him. But Raider, with his Fulton County, Arkansas, dirt-scratcher upbringing, which a lifetime in the Far West had only intensified, was hardly the man to hobnob with royalty.

Raider's inbred American ideas of equality and classlessness were confusing to Doc. As an American, Doc believed in them too—at least intellectually. But when it came to worthiness, he was a firm believer that class and breeding would always tell, which had often caused considerable friction between himself and Raider, who saw himself as the champion of the common man. Yet, oddly, they worked well together. When the chips were down, they were a smoothly functioning team.

Well, that was obviously it, Doc thought. Raider was along because the two of them were partners. Had been partners for years. With Doc's brains and cultural superiority, and Raider's brawn and skill with a gun, they were not all that bad a choice for the job.

When the summons had arrived from the head office in Chicago, they had been in Missouri, involved in the agency's eternal hunt for its number one nemesis and mortal enemy, Jesse James. Jesse and his gang had become an obsession with Raider and Doc's employer, the Pinkerton National Detective Agency. The agency had once even gone so far as to plant a bomb in Jesse's family's home, in the hope that Jesse or his brother Frank might be there when it went off. They hadn't been, and the only result of the ensuing blast had been to kill a little boy and to blow off Jesse's mother's arm. That hadn't made the agency any friends.

Neither Doc nor Raider was sorry to be pulled off the hunt for the James gang. Not that they subscribed to the popular fiction that Jesse James was a modern Robin Hood. They knew him for what he was—a cold-blooded thief and killer. Having seen the bodies of more than one unarmed man that Jesse had gunned down, they'd have been happy enough to see him hang. But the obsessive nature of the hunt was getting them down.

That day, they had been nervous, as usual, as they started together up the stairs to the agency's Chicago offices. They knew, of course, that whatever the assignment might be, it would involve them in danger, but that was not what made them nervous every time they went up those stairs. No, it was old Allan Pinkerton himself who made them nervous. He was, as Raider had put it, "one tough old coot." Not that Doc would have phrased it quite that way, but he knew what Raider meant.

Allan Pinkerton had founded his detective agency more than twenty years before, in the 1850s. At the time, the United States had been essentially without police forces, especially in the western parts of the country. Of course, there were county sheriffs, but they were often either corrupt or incompetent. Back then, the United States was a lawless land, where justice tended to be private. Bandits and outlaws operated fairly openly, without much fear of being caught.

Allan Pinkerton, Scottish-born, and in his earlier years a champion of the workingman—which was the reason he had fled Great Britain, only a jump ahead of the noose because of his labor union work—was determined to bring some law and order to his adopted land. Within a few years of the founding of his agency, he had an awesome reputation as a scourge of the lawless. He also had a reputation for personal bravery. A number of times he'd overpowered desperate and dangerous men in hand-to-hand combat.

More importantly, he had built an efficient, effective organization. He had operatives and informants all over the republic, and had built up an impressive rogues gallery that was invaluable in tracking down and capturing the men he was after. His agents were trained to be methodical and patient. When Allan Pinkerton's organization went after someone, they usually got him. Which was one reason Pinkerton felt so frustrated at being unable to bring Jesse James and company to justice.

Strong men trembled at the mention of Pinkerton's name, and Doc and Raider, who had faced death dozens of times and never blanched, blanched now as they opened the door and walked into the offices of their employer.

And were shocked by what they found. They knew, of course, that the old man had been sick, but the memories, the images of the past, were still strong enough for them to hope that he would once again be himself.

Old Allan had had a stroke a few years before. After a number of months of complete helplessness, he had rallied enough to once again take over the direction of his agency, but more recently he'd started the long slide back downhill. When Doc and Raider entered the office, they were barely able to recognize, in the hunched, trembling figure who sat at Pinkerton's massive desk, the powerful, energetic man who had for so long run the nation's premier private detective agency. Only the intensity of old Allan's gimlet eyes over his thick Old Testament beard reminded them of who he really was.

He looked up as Doc and Raider approached his desk. His eyes glittered and his lips writhed as he tried to speak. Pinkerton clearly had something of import to say to his two top agents. They both leaned close, straining to hear. "Raider," Pinkerton finally wheezed, his thick Scottish burr still strong, "Yeer a week behind in yeer daily reports.

Ye know that it's regular habits that make the regular man. I'll not be havin' an operative o' mine—"

He went into a fit of weak coughing. Doc stepped close and pounded him on the back—which only brought Doc to the old man's attention, temporarily getting Raider off the hook. "An' ye, Weatherbee," Pinkerton said, his voice stronger now. "Ye were way over on yeer expense account. Way, way over. Ye know that any expenditure over fifty dollars has to be approved by the main office—"

Another fit of coughing. "Damn, damn, damn," Pinkerton half-whispered when it had passed. "This is no way to live."

Doc and Raider were embarrassed and touched. They loved the old curmudgeon, despite their awe of him, and hated to see him in this condition. They scuffed their feet self-consciously until old Allan was able to speak again. "Go on inta Wee Willie's office," he said. "The boy'll ken ye what it is that ye're to do."

Doc and Raider nodded, then entered an office off the main office. Willie, the "boy" old Allan had referred them to, was his son, William Pinkerton. Big William, as some called him, a brawny man in his thirties with a round, florid face, bulging eyes, and a thick mustache, was a somewhat larger version of the old man in his youth. He radiated a rather crude strength and energy, mostly through the flat fierce stare of his protuberant eyes. "Raider... Weatherbee," he boomed out. "Glad you could get here so quickly."

The two operatives eyed one another warily. They were more accustomed to hearing how slow they'd been. "I've got a ticklish assignment for you," Big William said. "One that will take a lot of diplomacy."

More raised eyebrows from Doc and Raider, and Doc's first questioning of what Raider was doing here if diplomacy was involved. Raider was definitely not known for his sense of tact.

"As I said, it's ticklish," Pinkerton continued. "Normally the State Department would handle a situation like this, but they've run into resistance. You see, he has this penchant for traveling incognito, or thinks he travels incognito."

"How's that?" Raider broke in, much less in awe of Big Willie than he was of his father. "He travels in a what?"

Doc sighed tiredly. "No, Raider. Incognito means you travel anonymously, not inside a cognito. Oh hell, that won't work either. I mean, he doesn't want anybody to know who he is. Which I suppose makes some sense, because I certainly don't know who he is." Doc shrugged elaborately in Pinkerton's direction, as if trying to let his employer know the handicaps he worked under.

"Why, you smarmy little shit," Raider snarled, having picked up Doc's inferences concerning his intellectual capacity. "How'd you like to start chewin' on a knuckle sandwich?"

"That'll be enough...both of you," Big Willie snapped, and there was enough of the power of the old man in his voice to instantly quiet his two operatives.

"Now," he said, sitting down at his desk, "maybe I'd better explain it from the beginning. This important visitor I'm talking about is the Grand Duke of Wittgenstein. It seems he's taken it into his royal head to go on a hunting expedition out west."

"The Grand Duke Wilhelm?" Doc broke in. "Yes, I've heard of him. But why all the fuss? Lots of European nobility make a regular habit of visiting the West."

"Well, I wouldn't think I'd have to tell you, Weatherbee, but there's tension in the Duke's part of the world. Wittgenstein has enemies. First there was that old hardnose Metternich, and now there's this new troublemaker ...what's his name?"

"You mean Bismarck? Count von Bismarck?"

"Yes, yes, of course. He's intent on building all those little German states up into one big German state, run, of course, by his own country, Prussia. They're really going at it hammer and tongs, those Prussians. You remember what they did to the French in '70, and then to Denmark, when they took Shleschwig-Holstein away from 'em. They've got everybody around 'em scared to death. There are only a few independent German states holding out now, and of course, one of them is—"

"—Wittgenstein," Doc finished for him. "Which means that this Grand Duke Wilhelm is in a key position."

"Exactly. And I think he's an idiot to even consider leaving his country at a time like this, but royalty will be royalty. Which is where we come in. The Secretary of State wasn't all that happy about the Grand Duke coming over here and disappearing somewhere out West. If anything were to happen to him, there would be heavy repercussions. A lot of people, particularly the French and the English and the Russians, are very much interested in keeping Wittgenstein independent. Well, hell, they don't really give a damn about this Grand Duke Wilhelm and his little postage-stamp country, but as long as it's independent, Prussia's opportunity for further expansion will be slowed down a little."

"Well, then," Raider put in sagely, "it wouldn't surprise me none at all if these Prussian fellas you're talkin' about would like to see this Duke end up as a meal for a grizzly."

Doc did a mock double take. "Why, Raider," he said sweetly, "your grasp of world politics is positively overwhelming."

A glare from Raider.

"Gentlemen!" William Pinkerton said warningly, "we'll have no more of this squabbling. Now, as I was saying, the State Department would rather not have the man here at all, but how do you say that to the head of a sovereign nation? Especially when the Duke absolutely insists on coming? About the only thing they were able to accomplish is to talk him into hiring local guides for his hunting trip. In fact, they made it a condition of the trip."

Raider sighed. "An' I guess we're gonna be those guides."

"That's the plan," Pinkerton said. "Of course, you'll be more bodyguards than guides. I suppose the Grand Duke knows that too, but I think it'll make everyone involved happier if we maintain the fiction."

"Me? A hunting guide?" Doc burst out, clearly aggrieved.

Raider grinned. "Careful, ol' son. You might actually end up doin' some honest work for a change. I'll tell you what—you do the skinnin' an' I'll do the trackin'."

"It's not a laughing matter," Pinkerton cut in. "Your job is to protect the Duke. In other words, to see that he makes it back to Wittgenstein in one piece. That's your responsibility, boys, there's no getting out of it. Just hold one thought in your heads; concentrate on one thing: *Keep the man alive!*"

CHAPTER TWO

Their employer's final charge was fresh in the minds of the two Pinkerton operatives as they neared the wharf where they had been told the Duke's yacht would be moored. It was there all right, a long, low, graceful three-masted steam-sailor with fore-and-aft rigging. There was one single smokestack just forward of the main cabin, and high paddle wheels amidships on either side. The hull was black, highlighted by the bright brass of the portholes lining its sleek sides. While there was a certain amount of giltwork decorating the smokestack, paddle wheels, and deckhouses, it had been kept within tasteful bounds.

"What a beautiful ship," Doc murmured. "What I wouldn't give to be on board her, sailing to some exotic foreign port."

He became aware, then, of the lack of something he'd expected to see. "Oh no!" he groaned. "The barouche hasn't arrived yet. Damn it all, Raider, I told you we should have accompanied it here. If the driver gets lost . . ."

"Wasn't no way you was gonna get me in that fancy-dan rig," Raider said. "Hell, not even no self-respectin' dance-hall whore'd ride in a sissy contraption like that."

"Maybe you'd like to carry the Duke into town on your back," Doc snapped.

Both men were so intent on their castigation of one another that they failed to notice that they were not alone on the dock. Three seedy-looking longshoremen were lounging lazily against the side of a warehouse. Bored, with no work to do at the moment, their piggish little eyes lit up when they noticed the newcomers. "Well, damn my ass," one of them said loudly. "Looka the dude an' the clodhopper."

Doc paid them no attention, but Raider whirled toward the three men. Normally he'd have ignored such trash, but the man's words had cut him to the quick. Clodhopper? Farmer? No self-respecting horseman could accept a slur like that. "You say somethin', sewer-mouth?" Raider grated, taking a step toward the man who'd spoken.

With Raider's glittering black eyes fixed unwaveringly on him, the longshoreman began to suspect that maybe he'd made a strategic error. But there was no way he could back down in front of his cronies. "Yeah, country boy. I said somethin'." He turned toward the other two, grinning. "Jeez . . . smell the manure? I think the bastard's got it in his hair."

Raider just kept walking toward him.

"Raider!" Doc called out sharply. "No trouble. We can't have any trouble here . . . Raider?"

But Raider continued advancing. The longshoreman, certain now that he had indeed made a very serious mistake, tried to save the situation by lunging forward and taking a swing at Raider. Raider simply reached up with his left arm and stopped the blow in midair. Then, slipping his left hand downward, he used it to seize the longshoreman by the throat, while at the same time driving his open right hand into the man's groin. The longshoreman was already screaming when Raider raised him up into the air, holding him by the throat and the crotch, and tossed him into the filthy harbor water not far from the Duke's yacht.

Doc had rushed forward to try to stop Raider, but one of the other longshoremen mistook it for an attack and lunged at Doc. Doc, barely taking his eyes off Raider, who was at the moment in the middle of hurling the first man through the air, rapped the heavy silver head of his walking stick against the second man's kneecap. Excruciating pain lanced through the man's leg. Howling, he staggered to the side. Doc reversed the walking stick and, pushing the sharper end against the man's chest, toppled him off the dock into the water next to his companion.

The third man, perhaps mulling over the old adage about discretion being the better part of valor, scuttled away down the dock, looking back fearfully over his shoulder, while his friends swam, spluttering and cursing, toward a ladder about forty yards away.

The two Pinkertons were surprised by a sudden buzz of conversation from the deck of the yacht. Looking in that direction, Raider and Doc saw a party of three, two women and a man, the women very elegant-looking, looking in their direction.

"Now you've done it, you idiot," Doc said to Raider. "You've made us look like a couple of damned thugs."

"Don't sound like it to me," Raider said, grinning up at the deck. The well-dressed little group was now applauding. "Well done, sirs," one of the women called out gaily.

Raider, grinning even more widely now, might have answered, but Doc kicked him sharply in the shins, and while his partner was hopping on one leg, muttering sulfurous curses under his breath, Doc studied the little group on the deck more closely.

The two women were quite lovely. One was a brunette, tall and slender, but with a hint of well-placed fullness beneath her modish clothes. The other was a blonde, and quite unembarrassedly lush, with a richness of breast, hip, and buttock that no amount of clothing would ever be able to hide. The man was apparently a sailor, perhaps—from the appearance of his clothing, a petty officer. "Oh, it was nothing, really," Doc replied, downplaying the incident. "But may I ask, is the Grand Duke Wilhelm of Wittgenstein aboard?"

"Why, yes, he is," the brunette answered. "May I ask who you might be, sir?"

Doc had walked a little closer to the ship. The brunette was above him, perhaps a little more than fifteen feet away. The sound of her voice, low, melodious, cultured, with the hint of an accent, flooded into him like warm summer sun. Looking up into large hazel eyes slightly tilted up at the corners, he knew he was in trouble. "I'm . . . I mean we . . . the two of us . . . my partner and I . . . we're from the Pinkerton National Detective Agency. We're here to, uh . . . well, guide the Duke. We, uh . . ."

Lost in near speechlessness, hating the way he must be sounding as he slid deeper and deeper into the depths of those lovely eyes, Doc finally had the sense to shut up. "Well, you're here at last," the brunette said. Oh, that wonderful voice again! "We were expecting you. If you and your friend would care to come aboard . . ."

Doc leaped up onto the gangway, which caused Raider to miss the kick he had aimed at Doc's backside, in retribution for that sharp rap in the shins. Overbalancing, Raider nearly joined the two longshoremen in the water, but, catching his balance at the last moment by desperately grasping at the gangway railing, he followed his partner up onto the deck . . . and found himself staring into the sky-blue eyes of the blonde woman. Large, ingenuous eyes, set in a face of porcelain perfection, which included richly bowed lips of the deepest carmine, and one of the loveliest little noses Raider had ever seen.

"Oh, sir," she said. "That was wonderful, the way you handled that bully. I must say, though, you did pick him up in the most unusual manner. I mean . . . it must hurt so for a man to be seized . . . there."

Raider vainly fought the intense blush that darkened his already rather dark features. The girl's innocent blue eyes looked into his disingenuously for another few seconds, then suddenly brimmed over with laughter. "Oh, Willie," she said to the petty officer, giggling, a giggle which ran Raider straight through the heart. "He's actually blushing. And after such incredible boldness."

Doc, sensing that the situation was getting out of his control, turned to face the brunette. "Uh . . . if I may introduce us, ma'am. My name is Weatherbee . . . Doc Weatherbee. And this is my partner, Raider."

She gave the slightest of bows. "I'm Emma," she said in that marvelous voice, "Countess of Vorburg." She turned toward the blonde. "And this is Sophie."

The blonde nodded. Doc barely had eyes for her, although Raider was ogling her helplessly. "If you would be so kind as to tell the Duke we're here," Doc said.

"Well of course, Dr. Weatherbee," Emma said, and when she turned toward the petty officer, Doc knew he'd placed his foot in it. Willie? The blonde, Sophie, had called him Willie, and now Doc remembered how Raider had threatened to call the Duke Willie.

"Your Highness . . ." Doc started to say, but the Grand Duke Wilhelm of Wittgenstein cut him off in midsentence.

"See, Emma?" he burst out, grinning from ear to ear. "I told you it would work. It's clothes that make the man."

Doc was now paying a great deal more attention to the man he had thought a simple sailor. The Duke—and Doc saw now from his bearing that he had to be the Duke— was much younger than either he or Raider had expected —probably in his middle or late thirties. He had a wide face which was almost boyish except for thick blond mustaches, waxed and curled up at the ends to form two sharp spikes. His blond hair was cut fairly short, although a small cowlick fell down over his broad forehead. Like Sophie, he had blue eyes, but not nearly so large, nor tilted up at the ends. The Duke's eyes were sparkling with merriment as he tugged at his thick blue petty officer's jacket. "It fooled you, didn't it?" he said to Doc. "You see,

I like to travel . . . how do you say . . .?"

"Incognito," Raider filled in. Doc turned to stare at his partner. Raider looked down modestly. "It means, kinda like travelin' without nobody knowin' who you are."

"Exactly," the Duke said animatedly, beaming at Raider. Only Doc could see the malicious triumph in his partner's eyes.

There was a sudden clatter of horse hooves from the dock. Doc turned and saw an elegant open coach pulling up near the gangway, drawn by four matched grays. "I, uh, see that our transportation has arrived, Your Highness," Doc said. "We've arranged for a suite at the best hotel in New York. If you'll have the baggage brought on deck . . ."

It was Sophie who saw to the baggage, and she did it with love. She likes having things, Doc decided. All Raider noticed was the way the girl's lovely body moved inside the stylish gown she was wearing. It was a European gown, and cut much more daringly than anything Raider had ever seen outside a dance hall. Seeming oceans of creamy décolletage bounced and jiggled before his entranced eyes, and he knew he was in love.

There was no way possible to fit the mountain of luggage that had piled up on the yacht's deck into even as large a vehicle as the big barouche parked on the dock. Doc finally arranged to have a wagon and teamster sent later. "We are, of course, traveling as lightly as possible," the Duke said, pointing to the luggage, which rose in a mound nearly six feet high and ten wide. "Of course, I had to bring some necessary comforts for the women, but otherwise I intend to live the simple life of an outdoorsman while I'm in America. This is, after all, a hunting trip."

Both Doc and Raider tried very hard to tell if the Duke was joking. They finally decided that he was not. "And now, on to the hotel," the Duke said ebulliently. "Just the five of us now, of course. The servants will be along later."

The Duke strode off toward the waiting barouche,

Sophie and the Countess Emma trailing along behind. Apparently, where royalty was concerned, it definitely was not ladies first.

"Servants?" Raider muttered to Doc as they followed the royal trio. "What the hell does he think we're gonna be huntin'? Goddamn elephants in India?"

CHAPTER THREE

The Duke sat in the middle of one of the barouche seats, Emma on one side of him, Sophie on the other. Raider and Doc sat on the opposite seat, facing them. The Duke and the two women were quite animated during the trip into town, obviously enjoying the new sights. Doc noticed that the Duke was holding Sophie's hand, and the way she swayed toward him suggested that they shared something more than innocent friendship. Doc noticed that Raider had noticed too. He looked like a sick dog.

Doc began to wonder about Emma, Countess of Vorburg. There was an easy warmth between her and the Duke. Was she, also, like Sophie . . .?

Where royalty was concerned, one could never be certain. Doc felt a twinge of jealousy, then mentally cursed himself for a fool. After all, she was a countess, damn it! And he made his living chasing bandits.

They had to pass through the seediest part of the city to reach the Duke's hotel. Doc had hoped to keep talking, and thus divert the attention of the Duke's little party from their sordid surroundings, but to his surprise, the Duke was fascinated by the squalor. "Interesting place, New York," he said more than once. "Nothing at all like Wittgenstein."

When they began to pass a number of seedy bars and saloons, the Duke asked Doc to stop the carriage so that he could get down. "But, Your Highness," Doc protested, "it's not very safe."

"Safe? Safe?" the Duke demanded. "My God, man,

aren't we on our way out to the wilderness to hunt wild beasts? I'd never imagined for a moment that this trip would be safe." He suddenly turned in his seat and pointed to one particularly grungy-looking place. "There! Let's go into that one!"

Doc groaned. The saloon the Duke was showing such interest in was the notorious Shang Draper's, one of the most vicious establishments in a city known for its viciousness. Doc thought quickly. "Your Highness," he said sotto voce to the Duke, "I'm thinking of the ladies. That place is . . . well, how should I put it . . . a house of ill repute. To take ladies inside would be, to say the least, somewhat indelicate."

The Duke nodded in agreement. "You're right, of course. But then, maybe later . . ."

Doc vowed that "later" would never take place. But he had learned something that would be useful to him in the future. Each time the Duke planned some harebrained scheme, the thing to do was to invoke the ladies. As long as they didn't know he was using them, of course. At least not Emma. She would certainly resent it. Sophie, on the other hand, had obviously overheard what he'd told the Duke, but rather than being shocked, she looked decidedly amused.

They reached the hotel with no further ado. The Duke appeared satisfied with his lodgings, the Royal Suite, and settled into the largest room—with Sophie. Emma took the other bedroom. Once the two Pinkertons were positive that their charges were securely in place, they finally relaxed, repairing to the bar for a much needed drink.

"This ain't gonna be fun," Raider said glumly over a whiskey. Doc, having downed half his brandy in one quick gulp, nodded just as glumly.

"That Sophie . . . guess there ain't no doubt she's the Duke's fancy woman," Raider muttered, eyes downcast.

"Mistress, Raider. She's called a mistress in the Duke's

elevated circles. Or, perhaps, by the more squeamish, his 'companion.'"

Raider suddenly brightened. "Well, at least she ain't his wife. I never did go in for chasin' other men's wives."

"Raider," Doc said warningly, "I hope you don't have some misguided idea of going after the Duke's... woman."

Raider's grin broadened. "Not any more'n you have about goin' after his sister."

"I . . . his sister?"

"Yeah. Sophie told me while you was havin' the trunks an' stuff taken care of. Emma's His Nibs' sister."

Doc had to stifle a sigh of relief. Well, at least things were now clearer, even if Emma remained a countess. "Damn it, I need a nap," he said. "I think we'd better get our rest while we can. I doubt we'll get much on the trip."

Doc and Raider were sharing a room down the hall from the Royal Suite. Doc hated sharing rooms, but the agency's budgetary restrictions—hell, Scotch tightness—seldom allowed him to have a room of his own, unless he made up the difference out of his own pocket. On his salary, that was easier said than done. Nevertheless, his tiredness overcame the choked gargling of Raider's snores. Raider never snored out on the trail, where the slightest noise might prove fatal, but he certainly made up for it when he was indoors.

Sometime later, how much later Doc couldn't tell, he was awakened in the middle of a dream in which the Countess Emma played a major and rather sensuous role. As he came awake he was aware that the real Emma's voice was coming through the door to his and Raider's room. "Dr. Weatherbee?" she was calling softly, in between taps on the door. "I have to talk to you."

Doc sat up in bed. Looking over, he saw that Raider had one eye open. He was grinning. "You sly ol' devil," Raider snickered.

"Shut your filthy mouth," Doc snapped. Then he was up and heading for the door. He had left his clothing on, except for hat, shoes, and jacket, and felt well covered enough to answer the Countess's summons. When he opened the door, he saw her standing in the hall, hands clasped tensely in front of her body. Doc looked at her for a moment, once again stunned by her quiet loveliness. No, it hadn't all been a dream.

"Dr. Weatherbee," Emma blurted worriedly before he could say anything, "I think I need your help."

He raised his eyebrows. "It's the Duke," she continued. "He's . . . well, he should have been back by now, but he isn't, and I'm worried."

"Back? He went out?"

"Yes. He said that he wanted to take a closer look at that horrible saloon he was so interested in. He told me he'd be back in half an hour, but its been over twice that long. Perhaps I should have said something to you earlier . . ."

"Raider!" Doc said sharply. "On your feet. The Duke's gone to Shang Draper's."

Raider, who had been studiously sleeping, sprang quickly to his feet. "Goddamn idiot!" he snapped. "Sure as hell has more balls than brains. Oops . . . pardon me, ma'am."

Unfazed, Emma stood just inside the doorway while both men finished dressing. She noticed the heavy swing of the .44 in Raider's coat pocket as he pulled the coat on. She watched Doc shrug into the shoulder rig for his .32. "Is it that bad?" she asked.

"Sometimes they never even find the bodies," Raider said grimly. "Not for years, till they dig up the foundations o' some old buildin' they're tearin' down. They say the West's lawless, but I say it's this miserable den o' thieves that takes the cake."

"All right, that's enough, Raider," Doc said sharply when he saw how pale Emma had become. "Don't worry. We'll get him back, Countess."

They left her then and headed out into the street, armed for bear. By the time they approached the saloon, they both felt a touch of fear—not for whatever danger they might find inside; they were used to that—but rather, they were paralyzed by the thought of possibly having to face their employers with the news that they had lost the man whom they were supposed to protect.

Imagine their relief, then, when, after pushing through the swinging doors of the saloon, they saw the Duke standing at the bar, glass in hand. However, their relief was short-lived. The Duke was surrounded by several men. Hard-looking men. Doc stared at one of them. "Damn, that's Jimmy Bates," he murmured to Raider. "One of the worst cutthroats west of the Mississippi."

He was referring to a rat-faced little man who stood facing the Duke. Bates was dressed in clothing he may have meant to be elegant but instead was merely garish, including a gaudy checkered red and green vest and maroon trousers. A battered, not-very-clean derby rode his bullet head. The other men with him—and the way they were standing indicated that Bates was the center of their little group—were a motley collection of thugs and bums —mean, big, and ugly as sin.

The Duke turned as the swinging doors banged loudly behind Raider and Doc. "Ah, Weatherbee . . . Raider. Rather glad to see you."

There was a tension in his voice which indicated that, despite the blindness brought about by his privileged upbringing, the Duke may have finally recognized the trouble he was in. There was no doubt in either Raider or Doc's mind that the men around the Duke intended to rob him. Or worse. "Your sister was asking after you, Your Highness," Doc said. "We'll take you back to the hotel."

He immediately realized that he'd made a mistake referring to the Duke as "Your Highness." The predatory gleam in the eyes of Jimmy Bates and Associates increased to a high glitter.

"Hey, don't I know you?" Bates said to Doc. "Yeah. You're that fuckin' Pink, Weatherbee."

Doc nodded. He and Bates had had a run-in a few years before, which had ended with Bates going to prison over a robbery he'd committed. Bates moved away from the bar, toward Doc. "Yeah, been waitin' to meet up with you again, Pink. Been waitin' a long, long time."

The action exploded then, and amazingly, it was the Duke who started it. He had a large stein of beer in one hand, and he suddenly swung it hard against the head of the man closest to him. The mug shattered in a shower of beer foam, broken glass, and blood. The man who'd been hit went down like a poleaxed steer.

Bates's hand darted into his coat pocket. Doc saw the gleam of metal from the butt and top rib of a revolver, but his own hand was already inside his suit jacket, and before Bates could bring his piece up to stomach level, Doc had shot him in the chest, just left of center. Bates collapsed like a puppet whose strings had been cut. He virtually melted down onto the floor.

Doc turned. A man behind the Duke had produced a long thin knife and was now holding it poised above the Duke's back. A stupid way to use a knife, Doc thought as he shot the man through the side of the head.

After that he couldn't shoot anymore, because the Duke was too intermingled with his attackers. Doc rushed forward, along with Raider, clubbing with his revolver, wishing for once that he'd listened to Raider and had brought along a heavier pistol. Then he remembered that he still held his walking stick in his left hand, and began laying about him with the heavy silver head.

Raider, meanwhile, had charged into the middle of the pack. His fists quickly laid out two men, one after the other. He noticed that the Duke was handling himself very well, which elevated Raider's opinion of the man. The Duke had one attacker down and was holding off another with a fine display of boxing skill, which would have been all right except that the Duke was fighting fair, and Raider knew that at least some of his attackers had to be armed.

One of them definitely was, and he was rushing straight at Raider, a long tapered-bladed dagger, the kind known as an Arkansas toothpick, held out in front of him. Raider groped in his right coat pocket for his .44. It came out partway, and then the hammer caught on the edge of the pocket. Raider couldn't work it loose, and now the man was thrusting with his Arkansas toothpick.

Raider dodged, the knife slicing through his coat. The heavy material tied up the man's blade for a moment. Raider, never one to look a gift horse in the mouth, forgot about his pistol for the moment and, reaching across his body, pulled his bowie knife from its sheath and swung it in a vicious arc, left to right. The massive blade caught his attacker's wrist, severing his knife hand from his arm. Staring numbly at the spurting stump, Raider's attacker stumbled backward, out of the fight.

Raider transferred the knife to his left hand, and this time managed to get his pistol out into the open. Thumbing back the hammer, he snapped a shot at a man pointing a pistol at the Duke. The heavy bullet took the man in the shoulder, spinning him around.

The thunderous roar of the big revolver stunned everyone in the bar. The attackers froze as they heard Raider thumb back the hammer to full-cock. "Anybody moves gets his fuckin' head blown off," Raider announced.

The few attackers still on their feet backed slowly away, hands in plain sight. Raider and Doc tracked them with the muzzles of their pistols. "Along the bar. Nobody move," Doc snapped. "Just stand there until we leave."

Doc and Raider waved the Duke toward the door, then backed out after him, pistols covering the men at the bar. Only when they were in the street did they uncock their weapons and put them away. "Come on, move your ass," Raider said rather democratically to the Duke. "We gotta make tracks."

"But certainly," the Duke protested, "we should do our best to find the authorities. After all, men were hurt back there. Possibly even killed."

"You bet your ass there was some men killed. An' they got friends, some of 'em those same, goddamn crooked authorities you're yappin' about."

"He's right, Your Highness," Doc cut in. "If we want to stay in one piece, we'd best put some distance behind us. If they can't catch us, I doubt anyone will even report what happened. It's that kind of place."

They made it out of the area without any further trouble. As they neared the hotel's ornate front door, such a different world from the world of Shang Draper's saloon, the Duke slowed. "My apologies," he said. "My idiocy nearly got us all killed."

Doc looked embarrassed. Raider merely nodded and grunted. "Well, you're learnin', tenderfoot," he said.

Doc wanted to tell Raider that he shouldn't be using quite those words to the Duke, but the Duke was looking grateful. Raider spit into a pile of steaming horse droppings near the sidewalk. "That's what counts out where we're headin'," he drawled. "You learn quick enough, then maybe you'll survive."

CHAPTER FOUR

The next morning they crossed the Hudson on a ferry. The baggage would follow later. Doc had been told that they were to pick up a private train in Philadelphia. He was certain that the Duke had it wrong, that it was simply a private railway car. Many wealthy travelers had their own railway cars, which they attached to the companies' trains.

The crossing of the Hudson thrilled the travelers. The Duke and the ladies made suitable sounds of awe over the Palisades, the mighty basalt cliffs that rise up on the New Jersey shore in great black vertical columns. Once they had reached the far side of the river, a coach took them to the nearest train station. Here there was no private car waiting, just a simple short-haul train, but the Duke and his women seemed delighted to be sitting in a rather grimy railway car with the hoi polloi: dusty farmers on their way into town, smelling of earth and pigs; businessmen; families—all quite democratically unmoved by the presence of obviously wealthy foreigners. This impressed the Duke. "You are free here," he said to Doc. "Yah. That is good."

Doc had noticed that the Duke, who normally spoke excellent British-accented English, tended to develop a slight German accent when he was excited. At such times, "good" tended to come out as "goot," and "just" as "chust." A rather irrepressible man, a man of enthusiasms, the Duke was quite often excited.

Doc was beginning to like him. Raider, initially hostile to this representative of the European class system, had warmed to the Duke since the fight in Shang Draper's.

27

While they were still at the hotel, Raider questioned the Duke about the way he'd laid into his attackers at the bar. The Duke—only half modestly—told him that he had studied for a while with a noted English boxer.

"Well, now, Duke," Raider said. "That boxin' stuff's all right for the ring, where there's rules, but if you wanna stay alive in a real fight, you gotta make up your own rules."

Intrigued, the Duke had let Raider give him some lessons in rough-and-tumble survival fighting. He learned practical moves such as the knee to the groin, fingers in the eyes, the head butt, and how to break a kneecap with a sudden kick.

Raider also instructed the Duke in the basics of fighting with a bowie knife. The Duke was impressed by the big weapon. Its blade was not only long but quite thick and heavy, made as much for chopping as for stabbing and slashing. "I am accustomed to the saber, of course," the Duke said, thoughtfully testing the balance of the bowie. "This is . . . different."

"Sure," Raider replied. "I used sabers a coupla times, when I was scoutin' Indians for the cavalry. They come in damn handy from on top of a horse, when you need the extra reach. But when you're in a tight spot and can't get to a gun, then it's real nice to be able to move in close, right inside. Once you're in there, if you got a good knife you can split the other bastard all the way from his wishbone right on down to his socks. Or up the other way. Course, a gun is always a better bet, as long as you got one on you an' don't hafta keep quiet while you're killin' somebody."

This lesson was performed in front of the ladies. Doc saw Emma go a little pale at Raider's graphic descriptions of death and mayhem. Sophie, on the other hand, seemed rather morbidly interested. Doc realized that the girl was growing more and more fascinated by Raider. He fervently hoped that this fascination did not take some form that would cause trouble for them all.

They arrived in Philadelphia that evening and checked into the town's best hotel. They were now traveling on the Duke's money, of which he seemed to have an inexhaustible supply. Doc and Raider were given a suite, with separate bedrooms, while the Duke and his ladies had an even larger suite next door. Doc, a lover of luxury, which he considered his just due, wallowed in a night of sybaritic sleep, savoring the satiny feel of the sheets, the softness of the bed, the richness of the room's abundant furnishings. Waking in the morning to a hotel servant's discreet tapping on his door, Doc ordered breakfast in the suite's sitting room: smoked salmon, shirred eggs, fresh fruit, and the best coffee he'd tasted in months.

Doc was half finished with his breakfast when Raider came shambling into the suite's living room. "God, I'm hungry," Raider said, yawning. He took a closer look at Doc's half-empty plates. "Not that junk, though. I wonder if they got any grits an' molasses?"

Doc gagged on a mouthful of salmon. "Born a peasant, die a peasant," he muttered, fortunately too low for Raider to hear. Raider tended to have a nasty temper in the morning, especially when he woke up in a room, instead of in the great outdoors. Under the open sky, the beauty of the morning, his favorite time of day, almost always brightened his mood.

It was ten before the Duke's party had gone through its morning rituals. With the ladies bulky in silks and satins, they set out for the special trainyard where they were to pick up their transport.

Along the way, the Duke asked dozens of questions about Philadelphia. "They say it's the cradle of your democracy," he said, "whatever that means."

"Well," Doc replied, "a lot of the early leadership during the War for Independence came from here."

Doc pointed out Independence Hall and other landmarks of the revolutionary struggle. The United States had, of course, ceased to be a revolutionary nation by the middle of the century, although for several decades after the Revolution the oppressed peoples of other lands, yearning for freedom and self-determination, had looked upon the new republic as a shining example of the struggle against injustice.

Now, finally a rich nation after decades of existing as a small, weak, poverty-stricken parvenu, and greedy for land and power, the United States, in this year of 1876, it's Centennial year, was as rapacious as any European power. The Duke, a student of politics and world history, offhandedly mentioned this to the two Pinkertons. Curiously, Doc put up the most struggle against this theory, while Raider, the champion of the underdog, ruminated thoughtfully about the war against Mexico and the continuing decimation of the Indian tribes.

When they arrived at the trainyard, the two Pinkertons discovered that it was indeed an entire train that had been put at the Duke's disposal—for an enormous sum of money, of course. It consisted of a medium-sized Baldwin engine with six driving wheels, a wood tender, and five cars, including the train crew's caboose.

The first car after the wood tender was the baggage car, a damned big baggage car, Doc thought, but not too big for the Duke's vast amount of luggage. The next car was reserved for the weapons and other hunting equipment and also served as Doc and Raider's quarters. They each had a tiny private sleeping room.

The third car was for the Duke and the two ladies. It was the largest car, highly ornate, with large rooms and luxurious furnishings. The walls were paneled in walnut, the floors covered by oriental carpets, the windows and fittings framed in gilt and red velvet. There was a considerable bar, plus a library with books in several languages. A small but excellent piano was tucked away in one corner. Quite a crowded space, but elegant.

The last car before the caboose was the servants' car. Less ornate, but comfortable enough, it provided space for the cook, a kitchen helper, two maids for the ladies, the Duke's manservant, and a general dogsbody for whatever work was left over.

The servants were already aboard and had prepared the living quarters. A cold collage of fish and meats with various breads and fruits had been laid out, in case the short trip from the hotel might have tired the ducal party. Champagne and chilled white wines were available. The Duke and the women sat down and demolished this rather copious repast, including a good deal of the wine. Doc, who had never quite gotten used to drinking during the day, watched in awe as the Duke and entourage stuffed themselves. "I'd always heard that Germans ate a lot," Doc murmured to Raider. "But to see it in the flesh . . ."

"Yeah . . . flesh," Raider muttered, his eyes devouring Sophie's rich, well-upholstered curves as she picked clean a roasted pheasant leg. "God, Doc, how are we gonna make this a real huntin' trip? I mean, it's like haulin' a cotton-pickin' hotel along with us. The animals are gonna run like hell, an' the Injuns are gonna die laughin'."

Doc surveyed the elegant room, the crystal, the fine silver, the rich food, but most of all he studied Emma. Amazing that she was so slender, considering the amount of food she tucked away. Pensive, he finally arrived at a judgment. "I like it, Raider."

"You would," his partner snorted.

A large wagon loaded with the baggage arrived while they were eating. While the various trunks, bales, and boxes were being stowed away in the baggage car, Raider went to his and Doc's car to check the weapons. What he saw did not please him. For the most part the rifles were of smaller European caliber, and in his judgment rather flimsily built for the hard use they would experience in the West.

The Duke arrived a few minutes later to find Raider rather amusedly looking over a stocky German single-shot rifle, obviously a short-range target piece. The metalwork was chased and adorned with rather gaudy engraving. A handsome enough piece, but when Raider raised the stock to his shoulder, he found the feel of the weapon decidedly clumsy.

"You do not like my guns," the Duke said half accusingly.

"Oh, they're pretty enough," Raider said. "But I understand everything's kinda small in Europe, includin' the animals. The land's kinda closed in, too. You don't get too many real distance shots. An' you don't hafta pack a rifle too far yourself, what with all your slaves . . . uh, servants, an' that kinda thing. But out West, huntin' ain't always so convenient."

Raider laid down the blocky rifle and picked up a beautiful shotugn. "The scatterguns, though, they're real fine pieces."

"That one's English," the Duke said proudly. "A Purdy. Do you like the balance?"

"Perfect," Raider replied, "for birds. But I kinda figure you'll want to go after somethin' a hell of a lot bigger'n a duck."

"Yes, yes, of course. But perhaps you could guide me in choosing some appropriate arms."

Happy to comply—he loved weapons—Raider accompanied the Duke into the city, to the shop of the best gun merchant in town. Raider had seldom had his hands on much money, but when he bought a gun, he always bought the best. Too many times his life had depended on his weapons. He might scrimp on food, clothing, and lodging, but never on personal armament.

For more than a century Pennsylvania had been a good place to buy some of the finest arms in America. Raider now increased the Duke's armory with two Sharps .45-120 single-shot rifles. "I like it better'n the .50-95," Raider said. "Throws almost the same weight bullet, but has a bigger powder charge. Can't beat it for long-distance shootin'."

He also bought a big single-shot Ballard, plus a Model 1873 Winchester lever-action rifle in .44-40 caliber for lighter work, along with a copy of his own Remington .44 revolver for the Duke. "You can swap the ammo between the pistol and the rifle," Raider said. "Means you don't have to carry two kinds. Great when you're in a fight. What I'm waitin' for, though, is that new rifle Winchester says they're bringin' out this year. They're gonna call it the Centennial. It's a hell of a lot more powerful than the '73. They're chamberin' it in .45-75. Slings one hell of a chunk o' lead one hell of a long way, an' it's a repeater, which is gonna give it a real advantage over the big single-shot guns."

The Duke fell in love with an elegantly made little Remington .41 derringer, and bought it for himself. For the women, he bought light rifles and small .32 revolvers.

"Good snake guns," Raider said tactfully, trying not to sneer at the little pistols.

On impulse, Raider bought Doc a .50-caliber Barnes single-shot boot pistol. "For when that popgun o' his bounces its beans off whoever he's aimin' at."

Thus outfitted, they took a carriage back toward the trainyard. The Duke had bought a cartridge belt and holster for his new .44, and rather self-consciously strapped it on before they started back. Raider, now that he was out of New York, was once again wearing his .44. "Tell me the truth," the Duke said, grinning like a schoolboy. "Don't I look just like one of your western desperadoes?"

Raider looked into the Duke's ruddy, open features, glanced at his fancy clothing and at the rather clumsy way he wore his pistol. "Sure," he said, grinning back.

The carriage had just turned into the trainyard when the attack came. Fortunately, Raider had already noticed movement behind a railway shack about forty yards away —quick, furtive movement. "Watch it, Duke!" Raider shouted, his right hand dropping toward the butt of his pistol.

Three men, dressed in dark clothing and all carrying pistols, ran out from behind the yard shack and headed straight toward the carriage. One of them was leveling his pistol at the Duke when Raider shot him through the chest. The man managed to fire one shot before going down, but the shot went high, the man's aim ruined by the heavy impact of the .44's big bullet.

As usual in a fight, Raider's mind was working quickly and coolly, as if everything were happening in slow motion. He had time to realize that the attackers were damned good; they were fanning out, presenting themselves as scattered targets. The two men remaining on their feet opened fire, which Raider had anticipated by rolling to the side. There was no time to get out of the carriage, hemmed in as he was by the guns and equipment they had bought. His fight would have to start and finish right here.

He pulled the Duke down next to him with his left hand, while snapping off two quick shots with his right. A near miss tugged at Raider's jacket. The Duke snarled something in German, then, shaking himself free, jerked out his Remington and opened up on the attackers.

It was the Duke's participation that saved the day. The first of Raider's two quick shots winged one of the surviving gunman, but had not put him out of action. Kneeling, left hand clasped against the wound in his side, the gunman continued firing.

As was customary with a single-action pistol, except when a fight was imminent, Raider usually left the chamber under the hammer empty to avoid accidental discharges. That meant that he now had only two shots left, with no time to reload. And he was facing two determined gunmen. One more miss and he would be in big trouble. If he'd only thought to load the weapons they had purchased before putting them into the carriage . . .

But by then the Duke had dropped the man on the far left, the slug from his .44 knocking him flat on his back.

After that, both Raider and the Duke's bullets tore into the kneeling gunman, killing him instantly.

Raider rolled off the far side of the carriage, shucking empties out of his pistol and reloading as fast as he could cram in the shells. With the Duke right behind him, he ran up to the fallen men, covering them with his reloaded pistol.

Two were dead. The man the Duke had shot was still alive, lying on his back, his chest soaked in blood. Raider could see that he didn't have long to live; his eyes were already glazing, his breathing was weak, and he was murmuring something mindlessly over and over again.

Raider leaned closer. At first the words meant nothing to him, then he realized that the man was repeating in German, *"Mein Gott . . . mein Gott in Himmel."* He died then, the breath sighing out of him in one last *"Gott."*

The Duke had also picked up the words. "So then," he said softly. "They have come all the way to America to find me."

"Who?" Raider demanded. "Who are 'they'?"

The Duke waited a moment before answering. "People who want to see me dead," he finally replied. "Powerful people."

Raider looked up at the Duke, who was still standing with his .44 in his hand, his face grim, a final curl of blue gunsmoke seeping from the pistol's barrel. Raider looked around at the dead men. "Well, they're gonna have to work for it."

CHAPTER FIVE

The sound of the shooting had, of course, carried some distance. By the time Raider and the Duke had driven the rest of the way to the train, Doc was running toward them, a shotgun in one hand. "What the hell happened?" he demanded.

"Three men. Real pros. Hit us when we were just drivin' into the yard."

At Doc's questioning look, Raider added, "Dead. All three of 'em."

"Any idea . . .?"

"Yeah. The kinda people Big Willie warned us about. People from over there, the old country, an' it wouldn't surprise me none if there was more of 'em hangin' around. I think we better get this show on the road."

Doc nodded, then went racing off to round up the train crew. Raider drove the rig up to his and Doc's car and began transferring the weapons he and the Duke had purchased from the carriage onto the train. Once aboard, he loaded each gun, then had the male servants distribute them between the Duke's car and Raider and Doc's. The servants were plainly frightened, but a few short sharp words from the Duke got them moving.

Sophie and Emma were in the sitting room of their car, both somewhat pale. The Duke had already told them what had happened, and both women were doing a good job of controlling whatever fear they felt. Raider was relieved. There was nothing worse in a crisis than being saddled with a bunch of hysterical females.

However, that didn't mean they had to be careless. "Get away from the windows," he said brusquely. "Sit down behind somethin' heavy."

Both women grew a little more pale, although Raider could see that Sophie was probably more excited than afraid. He took a good long look at the big blonde, cursing for the hundredth time that she was the Duke's woman.

Meanwhile, Doc was locked in fierce argument with the train's engineer. "I don't move this engine till I get the word from the yard master," the engineer said stubbornly. "That nabob we're haulin' around in this movin' French whorehouse may be a big man where he comes from, but I'm an American railroader, sport, an' I do things the American way. That means I listen to the yard master. As far as I'm concerned, he's king, an' your man's only a goddamn duke, an' a foreign one at that."

Doc ground his teeth at this display of reverse snobbism. "Doesn't the safety of your train mean anything to you?" he snapped.

"Sure, mister. An' you better believe that's all that means anything to me."

"Keep up with what you're doing, and you'll get your train, and the passengers, and probably yourself shot to pieces."

The engineer's eyes showed more interest now, plus a smidgen of nervousness. He had heard the shooting. "What the hell do you mean?" he asked belligerently.

Doc decided to embroider the truth a little. "I mean that there's a small army of German assassins out there, just waiting to hit your train. If you don't get this damned thing moving, we're all going to be sitting ducks. Now, isn't that a little more important than your yard master?"

There was one last play of stubbornness over the engineer's coal-dust and oil-stained features, followed by instant decision. "Right. We'll be on our way in five minutes. Already got steam up."

True to his word, five minutes later, after several loud

blasts on the train's whistle called the crew aboard, the train was moving. But not fast enough for Doc. They were still moving fairly slowly when they passed the scene of the attack.

Raider and Doc were in the main car with the Duke and the women. Loaded weapons were stacked all around. Despite Raider's warning to keep his head down, the Duke looked out the window at the bodies, which were still lying where they had fallen. "I'm getting an impression," the Duke said dryly, "that it's a custom in this country to shoot men daily and then just go on your way."

"Not at all, Your Highness," Doc replied somewhat stiffly. "Normally, we'd have one hell of a lot of explaining to do, both about those men lying out there and also about the men in Shang Draper's. But we have the agency behind us, you see, and they have a lot of influence. They'll see that the legal aspects of this mess are cleaned up."

The Duke nodded heavily. "Yes. Of course. And I see that no matter where one finds himself in this world, it is always the level of influence one controls that determines the final rules."

He sat down, staring at the wall. Doc sat opposite him. "I need to know more about the men who tried to kill you," he said. "Otherwise, we'll be working in the dark."

The Duke shrugged. "What can I tell you? They no doubt work for the Prussians—in other words, for Bismarck. I have refused to join their 'Greater German Reich,' therefore they want me out of the way. The rest is simple, is it not? Dead is as much out of the way as can be arranged."

"We'll see that it doesn't turn out that way, Your Highness."

The Duke shrugged. "Oh, it will. Eventually. They are too powerful, and Wittgenstein too small—and too proud. Or perhaps it is myself who is too proud."

There was a short silence, then the Duke stood up. "However, I will not let those people ruin my hunting expedition. This is a most beautiful and exciting land. I intend to enjoy it."

The seriousness had left his face, and his expression was once again open and cheerful. But at what internal expense? Doc wondered. Or maybe this was the real man, and the concerned, serious ruler the impostor. Whichever, Doc and Raider had a job to do: keep the man alive. But it had become more than just an assignment. Now that he and Raider knew the Duke better, a personal element had been added.

Apparently the three attackers had been alone. There was no firing into the train as it steamed slowly out of the yard. They made it out of Philadelphia without further incident. Once in open country, Doc and Raider felt more at ease. Here in the East there were so many rail lines that it would be difficult for an enemy to predict just where they might be heading. That was one of the many advantages of having your own train—you were quite free, within the rules laid down by the railroads.

The engineer hadn't merely been beating his gums when he'd talked to Doc about the yard master. If trains were not to meet head-on at high speed, there had to be some agreement as to who used what track, and when. Which would make it possible, after all, for a pursuer to eventually discover at least their general direction of travel. What they would have to do was determine that anew each morning. Of course, once out West, that would not work. There was only the one ribbon of track heading out over the plains toward the West Coast.

Time to worry about that later. Peace had returned to the train. The guns were placed in handy corners, still loaded but no longer so obvious. The general air of tension had faded, and the Duke and his women sat in their overstuffed chairs, gazing out the window at the landscape moving by. The train was now blazing along at over forty miles an hour, eating up track. Everyone found the speed a little disconcerting, but by tomorrow they would be far from

Philadelphia—and from whoever it was who was hunting the Duke.

Life aboard the train was quite pleasant. Raider and Doc moved regularly between their quarters and the Duke's, making sure that at least one of them was always in the Duke's car. They were all now much more in one another's company.

Which had its good points and its bad. Able to see so much of Emma, able to observe her as she performed the day's small, routine activities, Doc grew more and more fascinated by her. And more and more infatuated. For his part, Raider spent hours at a time within sight of Sophie. Constantly faced with the instinctive sensuousness of her every movement, he soon began to suffer pangs of simple, old-fashioned, unrequited lust.

However, he made no move to do anything about it, both because Doc kept an eagle eye on him and because she was the Duke's woman. That was quite a serious thing. He and the Duke had now fought side by side. One did not betray a fellow warrior. At least, not so that he'd know about it; and, considering the close proximity in which they were all living, Raider could not see how the Duke would fail to know. If anything ever happened.

The situation solved itself on their third day out, for, if Raider was captivated by Sophie's lush charms, she was equally hungry for what she considered his savage maleness.

Once on their way, they proceeded slowly, often stopping the train on isolated sidings so that they could get down from the cars and explore the countryside. They had been passing through Indiana, heading into Illinois. There was still a great deal of thick forest along the right-of-way, although the influx of settlers over the past fifty years had cleared much of the land, turning it into farms.

On this third day they stopped the train at an abandoned siding. It was so isolated a spot that the engineer could not imagine why a siding had been placed there at all. Thick, old-growth forest, obviously unlogged, stretched away on both sides of the track. They stayed all of that day, the entire night, and half the next day, the Duke using the time to practice in the forest with his new guns.

Although he liked the Duke, Raider discovered that he did not like being near him when he hunted. Showing a European nobleman's insensitivity toward the world of nature, the Duke shot anything that moved, and usually left it lying where it fell. Raider had little use for hunting for its own sake. He shot game when he needed the meat, and did not understand men who hunted merely to kill. Their second day on the siding, Raider maneuvered the situation so that it was Doc who got stuck with the Duke during his most recent shooting practice, while Raider wandered off into the forest on his own.

He was not that fond of the eastern forest; he preferred the openness of the West. There was something rather spooky about these thick woods. A part of him kept expecting to see a witch or a spirit appear from between the massive trunks of the older trees.

And then one did. Raider had been wandering along, hands in his pockets, when his trail-trained ears picked up a small sound from behind him: the scrape of a foot against stones. Raider spun around and was slapping gun leather when a familiar laugh froze his hand on the butt of his Remington.

It was Sophie. Walking out from behind a thick stand of bushes, she smiled at him. "I am so glad to find you here," she said. "I am very nervous about being in the woods by myself. The Duke said that there might be bears here. Or Indians. I don't know which would be worse, but you will protect me, won't you, Raider."

"Well, ma'am, I don't hardly think you'll find any Indians around these parts. But, yeah, I s'pose there's bears."

Sophie shivered rather theatrically. "Willie did warn me not to go into the woods without either you or Dr. Weath-

erbee by my side. I like Dr. Weatherbee very much, but
. . . you are so much the stronger."

Sophie ran a frankly appraising gaze over Raider's powerful frame. There was heat in her eyes, and Raider began
to grow nervous. "Well, ma'am . . ."

"Please, call me Sophie. And . . . Oh! Is that water over
there?"

She was looking through a screen of willows toward a
pond. There was a small clearing around the pond. Sophie
wiped a hand across her brow. It was a warm, humid day
and her skin was glowing. "How wonderful it would be to
swim," she said gaily. "Come with me . . . let's do it."

"Well, ma'am . . ." Raider said again, just as lamely as
the first time. He wished he could think of something else
to say.

"No, I asked you to call me Sophie," she corrected as
she began to unfasten the many buttons that held the front
of her dress together.

"Hey! Now wait a minute!" Raider blurted.

"Oh, Raider, don't be childish. We Europeans are not so
shy as you Americans. I really do not mind you being here
at all."

She smiled a smile that made Raider shake in his boots.
"Actually, it makes it all that much the more . . . how
should I say it? Exciting!"

By now she had unbuttoned the top of her dress, baring
nearly all of two very large and very firm-looking breasts.
Raider's breath caught at the sight of the small pink nipples
that rather incongruously capped all that smooth white
flesh. "Help me with my dress," Sophie said, laughing
gaily.

Raider, hardly a stranger to the female form, decided
that this last was an order, perhaps a part of his agency
duty. Anyhow, it wouldn't do any harm to just help the
lady out with her clothes. Or in this case, out of her
clothes.

Raider rather clumsily aided Sophie as she slid the tight-fitting dress down her body. She was wearing nothing beneath it, not one scrap of cloth, which made sense since it was such a warm day, but it was hardly the custom of the times. Most women wore under their outer clothes a nearly impenetrable mass of heavy, clumsy underclothing. None of that for Sophie. She was either a very unconventional young lady or had planned this whole thing very carefully before leaving the train.

The last of the dress slipped to the ground, leaving Sophie quite naked. She glanced back at the water, actually turned for a minute as if to indeed go swimming, but then turned again to face Raider.

Only a few feet separated them. Raider stood absolutely still, knowing that he should look away from Sophie but unable to. He was, however, not quite as still as he intended to be. As his eyes drank in Sophie's nakedness, a certain part of his anatomy was stirring and growing.

Sophie was not unaware of Raider's anatomical reaction. She looked down his body, her eyes opening wide. Suddenly she began to breathe very hard. All the laughter and gaiety vanished from her face, to be replaced by a look of the most intense yearning that Raider had ever seen, a naked hunger. "Ze swimming . . . ve vill do zat later," Sophie murmured. Her accent, always the strongest of the three Germans, had suddenly become much stronger.

She bent down to pick up her dress. Good, thought Raider dutifully, but not really meaning it, she's gonna put it back on. He too was aware of the growing presence lower on his body, and quite embarrassed by it.

But Sophie merely stretched her dress out on the ground and lay down on it, on her back, her arms stretched up toward Raider. "Please," she panted. "I am not very much good at waiting."

"Ah, shit," Raider muttered. This was more than a man could be expected to take. He knew that he should turn and walk away, but how was he going to tear himself away from so damned much woman?

He'd already noticed that her breasts, large as they were, had not lost their shape even though she was lying on her back. Now there was one hell of a pair of tits. And the rest of her! Those legs, for instance. She had spread them apart in open invitation, and beneath the golden vee of silky-looking hair that framed the juncture of legs and hips he could see more pink flesh. Wet flesh. Wet and shiny.

It occurred to Raider that it would be damned insulting to just turn around and walk off, leaving her lying there after she'd made it so plain she wanted him. And besides, there were the bears. . . .

"Arrgghhh!" Raider groaned helplessly, and then all reason drowned under the flood of his desire for the girl. She was so goddamned open about it all, in a sense almost innocent in the way she offered herself. He told himself not to be an idiot, not to turn down what was being handed to him.

Raider tore at his clothing. It seemed to take forever, but in a remarkably short time he was as naked as Sophie. *"Oh . . . Liebchen!"* she moaned as he fell on her.

Soft arms wrapped around Raider's neck. He moved his body in between Sophie's compliant legs, intensely aware of all that softness beneath him, the pillow of her breasts, her belly, those velvety thighs. Doc was always going on about how he liked skinny women, like the Duke's sister, but not Raider. Oh sure, he'd take on a skinny one if she was good-looking enough, but what he really appreciated was flesh, and with Sophie, he now had an amazing plenitude of flesh.

Their lovemaking was wild, fierce, demanding. Days of looking at one another without being able to touch had increased their mutual desire to a fever heat. Sophie whimpered in German. She panted and moaned, bucking upward so wildly that she nearly threw Raider from her. Yep. One strong, healthy woman.

He held on to the girl, pinning her down, which she loved, until the two of them had spent their passion in great rippling shudders of pleasure. He stayed on top of her for a minute or two longer, panting, still aware of all that soft firm flesh. He finally rolled onto his side, his ass grazing a patch of nettles. "Ouch! Goddamn it all!"

Sophie chuckled. "Now we must really go swimming," she insisted.

She led the way into the water, her white body gleaming in the dim light of the forest. They splashed together, laughing and fondling one another, until Raider began to grow nervous. The Duke was wandering around somewhere within this very forest. Maybe not very far away. Maybe he was standing behind a tree right now, watching them, his new Winchester in his hands. Maybe he was even looking straight down the sights at them. "I think we better get our clothes on," he said rather coolly to Sophie.

At first the girl was somewhat hurt by his coolness. Then she understood. "Ah . . . you worry about Willie."

"Yeah. I don't think he'd look on this too kindly. Might find it a little hard to understand."

Sophie laughed as she walked over to pick up her dress. "Oh, he would understand, all right. And probably not like what he saw. But he would not, oh, how can I say it? He would not be as excited and angry by this as you might think. I am, as you know, not his wife."

"He's married?"

"Oh, yes," Sophie said, and there was a slight note of hostility in her voice. "The Grand Duchess, damn her. No, I shouldn't say that. She's not a bad woman, quite kind to me, really. And of impeccable birth. That is, of course, of the utmost importance in dynastic marriages. But she is such a dry stick, religious to the core, and as dull as a prelate. Which, of course, is why the Duke likes to travel with me. I'm not dry at all, am I, Raider?"

Raider remembered the moist heat of her. "Nope," he said, grinning.

"Well, we have our roles, then, the Duchess and I. She is the breeder of little Grand Dukes. I am his source of companionship . . . pleasure . . . life."

She said it gaily enough, but Raider detected a note of bitterness beneath the surface lightness of the girl's words. "Yes," she continued. "Willie would be a little annoyed if he caught us. But then, I know that he likes and admires you. Maybe he even thinks of you as a friend, if a Grand Duke can have friends. And what does one do for one's friends but share their possessions?"

Another tantalizing glimpse of bitterness, and then the girl's normal light and cheerful mood returned. "Don't misunderstand, Raider," she said. "I do not regret my life. I would always rather be me than the Duchess, despite all her titles and status. I love pleasure, I live for it, I live for life, possessions, all that is sweet, and with Willie, I can have all of these things. At least for now, and maybe forever. I doubt that Willie will leave me penniless."

Raider had by now put his clothes back on. He watched as Sophie wriggled into her dress, fascinated by the way her body moved. But he was a little confused. Damn. Too bad he couldn't talk to Doc about this. Doc was good at understanding this kind of thing. But Doc'd bust a gut if he found out. "Well, I know one thing for sure," he finally muttered. "Glad I ain't no Duke. That kinda life is a little too complicated for this ol' Arkie."

CHAPTER SIX

It took only one more day to reach St. Louis. Here they were to cross the Mississippi, which would delay them at least two days. There was no bridge, and thus no railway track across the river. Usually, passengers continuing west crossed the river on a ferry and boarded another westbound train.

However, the Duke insisted that they retain the train they had started with, including the engine. Therefore, the entire train had to be ferried across the Mississippi's broad expanse on barges, a time-consuming operation.

The time factor did not bother the Duke in the least. After all, he was not really going anywhere specific, there was no timetable, no deadline, really no hurry at all. And while the train was being transported to the railhead on the river's west bank, there was a town to explore.

"St. Louis used to be the jumping-off point for settlers heading out over the plains toward the Oregon and Santa Fe trails," Doc told his trio of eagerly listening Germans as they detrained. "Of course, there were no railroads out here then; they made the crossing in big covered wagons. They had to brave the perils of hunger, bad weather, mountains, deserts, and most of all, wild Indians."

The ladies shuddered appropriately when Doc mentioned that dreaded word—Indians. Even the Duke looked impressed. Raider, however, snorted derisively. "The Injuns never bothered nobody much—till the Army an' the government, with their damned lyin' treaties, started robbin' 'em. Then they fought back. Some of 'em are still fightin' back, even though the smarter Injuns know they ain't got a chance."

"But surely—" Emma broke in.

"There ain't no surely about it!" Raider snapped. "Now that most o' the buffalo are gone, they ain't got nothin' to eat. Oh, sure, the government says they'll give 'em cows to butcher. That's in them damn lyin' treaties. But those politician crooks back East sell the beef contracts to fat-cat speculators who keep most o' the money an' most o' the beef for themselves. Hell, half the Injuns still left alive are starvin' to death. No, maybe more'n half."

"But that's barbarous!" the Duke burst out.

Raider snorted again, but before he could speak, Doc cut in. He felt a little deflated, realizing that he'd been talking like a pompous ass. "I'm sorry to have to agree, but I'm afraid Raider's right. I treated the matter too lightly. It's regrettably true that the Indian hasn't got a chance. It's an old story, as old as mankind itself. It's been going on for as long as there have been different ways for people to make a living, different ways of getting food. Whenever a more efficient culture comes along, it buries the less efficient. Why, if my history's correct, when our Indo-European ancestors got horses, they overran every other batch of people who didn't have horses, who just couldn't compete. It's the same with the Indians. They're basically hunters, and that's the root of the problem."

"Problem, hell," Raider growled. "Livin' free, livin' off whatever you can find, that's the only real way to feel a hunnert percent alive."

"Well, maybe for you," Doc said dubiously. For himself, he did not have much love for the hardships of the nomadic way of life—which often made him wonder why he kept returning to the West. "The thing is, hunting takes up a lot of land, thousands of acres to feed maybe a few hundred people, if they aren't to kill off all the game in the area, which is what they depend on. But on the other hand, thousands of farmers can live off that same land."

"Grubbin' in the dirt like hogs," Raider snorted derisively.

"Nevertheless, that's the root of the problem. Our countrymen don't really intend to rob the red man, but they see what they think is a nearly empty land out West, and wonder why the Indian won't share it with them, never realizing that the Indian *needs* all that empty land if he's going to keep on living as a hunter. And on the other hand, the Indian can't understand why the white man fences in the open range, cuts down the trees, fouls the water with industry, and kills off all the game. It's really a hopeless situation; there are no grounds at all for true understanding between such different ways of life. I suspect that the only Indians who will survive as Indians will be those who already have at least a rudimentary agriculture, like the Hopis and Zunis."

"Well," groused Raider, "they ain't so bad, for farmers. Don't tear up the land as much as others I can think of."

"Very interesting, Dr. Weatherbee," the Duke said thoughtfully. "And perhaps essentially correct. I hope, then, that we may have a chance to see something of this vanishing race before it disappears altogether."

"You may not find that very pleasant, Your Highness. Watching a people on the way to annihilation is not a pretty sight."

"It gets kinda dangerous, too," Raider said. "There's some pretty hard feelin's among the redskins. They don't seem to like us a whole lot."

"Poor people," Emma said sadly. "How unjust that such a noble race should perish."

"Don't go makin' no saints out of 'em ma'am," Raider said. "Some of 'em have always been mean as snakes."

"But—"

"They always were a rather savage people," Doc put in. "Their entire way of life was built around intertribal warfare, and in this they were often merciless. By our standards they're unbelievably cruel. To an Indian, torturing someone is fun. To be caught alive by warriors, and then turned over to the women . . ."

He let the thought trail away, watching with a certain amount of satisfaction as the three pampered Europeans shivered again. He himself was not overly fond of being around Indians; they scared the hell out of him.

He knew that Raider, on the other hand, liked Indians, which at first glance created a seeming contradiction, since Raider had fought and killed his share of Indians, even on occasion scouting for the Army. Once, when questioned about this, he'd said, "Hell, Doc, Injuns are people—ordinary human bein's just like us white men. Some are okay, others are real mean bastards. When I run across a buncha bad-ass redskins, like that bunch that wiped out that little settlement down along the Gila River that time, then I go after 'em. An' if the Army offers to go along, that's fine with me."

But then, Raider had actually lived with the Sioux for a time, and had obviously taken upon himself some of their beliefs. Fighting and killing were much more natural for Raider than for Doc.

However, for the moment the Indian problem was far away. St. Louis had grown up into quite a town, and Doc was looking forward to being in a city again. The train was quite comfortable, and the chef excellent, but to Doc, a dedicated gourmet, a single cook could never completely satisfy his gustatory greed. And in the Duke, he had discovered a fellow devotee of food. "There's a wonderful restaurant in St. Louis," he had told the Duke while they were still several hours short of town. "Tony Faust's Oyster House Saloon."

"Argghhh," Raider protested. "The kinda stuff they give a man to eat there'll turn your stomach." Which was not much of a feat with Raider; he had a notoriously touchy stomach.

"The oysters are delicious," Doc continued.

Raider made a face. "Slimy things. Like somethin' out of a farmer's nose."

"Raider! The ladies!" Doc snapped. Emma was indeed looking somewhat offended. Even Sophie shot Raider a disgusted glance, which surprised Doc, because the girl had been mooning around after the big Pinkerton for the past few days. Doc was relatively certain that they had made love; what else could the knowing, secret little smiles between them mean? Respecting his partner's hair-trigger temper, Doc had not said anything, and he would not, unless the Duke seemed on the point of finding out. But so far, fortunately, he seemed completely unaware of the liaison going on between his mistress and his hunting guide.

"But, the oysters aside, Your Highness," Doc continued, "the *pièce de résistance* at Faust's is something I'm positive you've never tried—quail on a bed of steaming sauerkraut."

"Sauerkraut," Raider snorted derisively. He might have embroidered on the subject, but to both Doc and Raider's surprise, the Duke bridled.

"I'll have you know, sir," he said in a voice that they had not heard him use before, "that sauerkraut is the national dish of Wittgenstein."

Raider wisely kept his mouth shut. He'd gotten to know the Duke well enough to realize that he might get away with stealing his money or sleeping with his mistress, but not with running down his little duchy. The Duke, normally a very mild-mannered man, was a lion where the name and welfare of his country were concerned.

While the train crew began the laborious job of overseeing the move across the river, the Duke's party and the two Pinkertons repaired to Tony Faust's Oyster House. Raider, eating a steak, watched with ill-disguised loathing as everyone else consumed several dozen oysters, then tore into the quail on sauerkraut. Between gigantic mouthfuls, the Germans mumbled their delighted appreciation of this unexpected culinary masterpiece. Raider shook his head. My God, how they could eat!

The Duke was so taken with the food that he insisted they stay in the connecting hotel, the Southern. Belching, the Germans led the way into the hotel's foyer, heads back, stomachs out, faces radiant.

Suddenly the Duke stopped in his tracks. Both Raider and Doc were aware of the sudden tension in the Duke's posture. Fearing another attack, they rushed forward, expecting to see more assassins dressed in black, guns in hand. Instead, they saw a single well-dressed man, hands free of anything more lethal than a slender gold-headed walking stick, rise from a chair and walk calmly toward the Duke. "My dear Wittgenstein," he said in German. Both Doc and Raider could understand that much.

"Von Bock," the Duke replied stiffly. "I might have known it was you."

After that the conversation became too complicated for even Doc to follow completely, although he was fairly certain that he heard some mention of Philadelphia.

Suddenly the Duke turned toward Doc and Raider and lapsed back into English. "I would like to introduce you to an old . . . acquaintance," he said, his voice very steady. He indicated the stranger. "This is Graf Otto von Bock—or, as you would say, Count Otto von Bock."

He then turned back toward the newcomer. "Von Bock, I would like you to meet Mr. Raider and Dr. Weatherbee, my . . . traveling companions."

Graf, or Count, von Bock was around forty years old, tall and powerfully built. His hair, dark blond in color, was cut very short, bristling upward. His mustaches were somewhat darker, very long, and twisted up at the ends into fierce hooks. When Raider and Doc were introduced, he raised a monocle to one eye and studied them silently, as if they were cattle he had been asked to purchase. "My pleasure . . . gentlemen," he finally said, with a sardonic emphasis on the "gentlemen."

Raider stared back just as coldly at von Bock. Here was the epitome of everything he hated: the aristocratic snob. Raider had noticed a deep scar running down the right side of the Count's face. "Glad to meet you too, Bock. Say, that's one helluva scar you got there. What happened? Somebody shove a busted beer bottle against your mug?"

Von Bock stiffened. Raider would have angered him less if he'd called him some foul name, but to denigrate his dueling scar, his proudest possession..."And just what might Mr.—what did you say his name was, Wittgenstein? Rudder? Just what does Mr. Rudder do?"

"Oh, Raider's a man of many skills, Count, but he is particularly talented with firearms. There are, or were, some men in Philadelphia who discovered as much—to their eternal sorrow. But then, perhaps you already know that."

"Perhaps," von Bock murmured. He had locked eyes with Raider and was trying to stare him down. He and Raider were pretty much of a size, the two biggest men present. Perhaps it was the instinctive challenge of size and strength that initiated the antagonism between them. They were practically sniffing one another out like a pair of dogs, the Count rather stiffly, Raider quite openly. It was the Count, however, who turned away first. "I'll see you later, Wittgenstein," he said, facing the Duke. "In fact, you'll probably be seeing quite a bit of me. I believe we are all staying here at the Southern. Are we not?"

Doc wanted to hear the Duke say no, that his party would be staying at another hotel, but the Duke was not about to back down. "Ah yes," he said dryly. "I forgot that you like sauerkraut too, von Bock."

CHAPTER SEVEN

Von Bock turned and walked away. The moment he was out of earshot, Doc turned to the Duke and began asking questions.

"He's one of Bismarck's jackals," the Duke replied. "I am not at all surprised to see him here."

"He's a jackal with pups," Doc said. Von Bock had joined four other men on the far side of the foyer. They had the same general appearance as the men who'd attacked the Duke in Philadelphia. They all wore dark, European-looking clothing, and had a purposeful, disciplined manner. "They look like military men," Doc said thoughtfully.

"Prussian officers," the Duke replied. "I know the type. All discipline, but with a total lack of what one might call the higher feelings."

"Come on," Raider broke in. "Let's either get the hell outta this hotel or get us some rooms."

"Surely they wouldn't try anything in a hotel lobby," Doc protested.

"With that bunch, I wouldn't bet on it," Raider replied grimly.

Once again they rented two suites with connecting doors, but this time the two Pinkertons made certain that at least one of them was always present in the Duke's suite. When night arrived, Raider insisted that they both sleep on couches in the suite's living room.

Doc spent a somewhat sleepless night, knowing that Emma was only a few feet away, on the other side of an unlocked door. He knew the door was unlocked because he had not heard her lock it. Had that been meant as an invitation? There was no doubt that she liked him, that she was perhaps even attracted to him. Fantasies of what he might find on the other side of that door filled his mind. Raider's adventures with Sophie had not made it any easier; they had merely shown the way. Raider himself was having little enough trouble sleeping. The bastard's sated, Doc thought bitterly.

In the morning the Duke insisted that they all go down to breakfast, rather than have breakfast brought up to them. The two Pinkertons tried to dissuade him, but the Duke was adamant. "I will not let that thug von Bock dictate the manner in which we live."

While the Duke's party prepared themselves for breakfast, Doc and Raider returned to their room to hold a conference. "Too bad about us being hung up here while the train's being ferried across the river," Doc said regretfully.

"What difference would it make? They know where we are an' how we're travelin'. They'd just follow. It'd be a lot easier for them to bushwhack us out on the open prairie."

"I wonder how von Bock found us so easily?"

"Why shouldn't he?" Raider snorted. "He knew the Duke was headed West, an' this is pretty much the only way you can get out West on a train. He's probably been camped here for days, just waitin' for us."

"He's got more men than we can easily handle—even after losing the three you downed in Philadelphia."

"Yeah. Even if we beat 'em, the Duke or the women might get hit. The agency'd bust a gut if that happened. Maybe we should try an' bushwhack 'em first. . . . Naw, we're stuck on that goddamn train. It's a lot easier for them to know where we are than for us to know where they are."

"And besides, Raider, von Bock's a Prussian count. There might be a lot of trouble if we just . . . bushwhacked him."

Raider grinned a savage grin. "That's the kinda trouble I don't mind. We gotta get rid of him and his men someway."

"Raider, don't you go doing anything—"

"Hey! Maybe I got us an idea! A way to get rid o' Von Bock kinda quiet-like."

"You mean . . . in the back?"

"Naw, Doc, you been readin' too many books. I mean, we can do it all real legal-like. You remember that big favor we did for the local law a coupla years ago?"

"No. Oh, yes—you mean for the sheriff."

"Yeah. Well, let's see if we can cash in on it."

The two Pinkertons spent another half hour working out the details of Raider's plan, and then it was time to head down to breakfast. The Duke and the women were ready, the women dressed to the nines. "This may be our last day in a civilized place," Emma said to Doc. "We wanted to look our best."

"You may be surprised just how fashionable some of the towns in the West can be," Doc replied, lost in admiration of the richness of her gown. The girl's slender upper body rose up out of the wide swell of the dress like an elegant flower. In contrast, Sophie was dressed quite daringly, with a décolletage that left little doubt as to the amplitude of her breasts.

With two such beautiful women, the Duke's party drew a lot of attention on the way down to breakfast. Doc felt his knees turn to jelly when Emma offered him her arm. As they walked down the staircase together, he was intensely aware of the vibrant warmth of her body. Even burdened by the heavy dress, she moved with a feline grace that hinted at both strength and passion. She smiled across at him; she was only an inch or two shorter. "You look a little tired this morning, Dr. Weatherbee. Didn't you sleep well?"

"How could I sleep, knowing you were in the next room?" he replied. The words just blurted out of him; he'd not meant to say them. He fought to control his expression, while at the same time searching Emma's face for the first signs of anger or embarrassment.

She did give a little start of surprise, then she smiled again. "I didn't sleep very well either."

My God, exactly how does she mean that? Doc wondered. However, they were now entering Tony Faust's; the Duke had insisted on oysters and sauerkraut for breakfast, which even to Doc seemed a bit much. But the Duke was the Duke, so into Faust's they went.

Surprisingly, it was already rather crowded, filled with men on their way to work who had stopped by for the mammoth breakfasts that Faust's offered.

The Duke's party ate heroically. Raider ordered a pound of steak, half a dozen fried eggs, and huge amounts of fried potatoes, along with coffee and bread.

The Duke, as he had threatened, was digging into a steaming mound of sauerkraut topped with fried oysters. Sophie insisted on having a steak to match Raider's, but with fried onions instead of potatoes. Emma had eggs and bread and fresh fruit.

Doc ordered shirred eggs with smoked salmon, quite a light repast compared to the mountains of food the others were consuming. Doc finished his food very quickly, then excused himself. "You're leaving us?" Emma asked, surprise evident in her voice. And maybe a little regret, too, Doc thought.

"I have some things to do," he said, bowing himself out. The Duke looked rather questioningly at Raider, who managed to avoid having to provide any answers by keeping his head close to his plate.

They were still eating when three of von Bock's men came into the restaurant. Raider immediately straightened up. He had been sitting between Emma and Sophie, but now he shoved his chair back a little. "Move away from me," he ordered the women.

They hesitated for a moment, then, noticing the new-comers, nodded. Pale, the women moved their chairs to the side, leaving Raider the elbow room that he suspected he might need.

The three Prussians saw them and altered their course so that they would pass close to the Duke's table. They were all big men, somewhat lesser carbon copies of von Bock, with the same close-cropped hair and flat blue eyes. All three bore dueling scars on their faces. "Damn if it don't look like they all been in the same fight," Raider muttered.

The Prussians walked up to the table. Raider noticed them glancing around quizzically. They're looking for Doc, Raider realized. They're wondering if maybe he's behind 'em somewhere.

But he wasn't, and now Raider saw cool speculation on the Germans' faces. They'd caught the Duke alone with only the one bodyguard. And there were three of them. They're gonna start a fight, Raider realized. And if the Duke got hit in the middle of it, well, that'd just be a sad accident.

All three men were armed; Raider could see the bulges beneath their coats. He looked quickly at the Duke. He wasn't wearing the new gunbelt for his .44, but Raider hoped he had the pistol in his pocket. Then he realized that the Duke's pockets were not large enough to accommodate the big Remington. No, he'd be on his own.

The Prussians walked right up to the table. All of them ignored the Duke for the moment; they knew that their real adversary would be Raider. As fighting men, they recognized another fighting man. The biggest of the three stood, legs braced, staring insolently down at Raider. "What is a common dog like you doing at a table with nobility?" he asked, sneering.

So that was it. They were going to try to goad him into a fight. After that, who knew in what direction the lead might fly? Raider resolved to play it carefully. He shrugged. "Well, this ol' dog's just here to bite the legs of any bums or thieves that try an' bother these here nobles."

The Prussian flushed a little. "I see that you have a lot of bark."

"Yeah. An' not the kind you find on a tree, neither, mister."

The two men stared intently at one another, but neither made a move. If there was going to be any trouble, each wanted the other to begin it. The Prussian particularly needed it to be that way, because the "accidental" shooting of the Duke that he had in mind depended on the fiction that he had been shooting back at Raider in self-defense.

His two companions were fanned out a little, which was bad for Raider. He might be able to get the big one and maybe one of the others, but then he'd have to spin all the way around to get the third. By then, it might be too late, either for himself or for the Duke.

Seeing that he wasn't getting anywhere with Raider, the big Prussian suddenly leaned over Sophie and stared straight down her cleavage. "Has anyone ever told you, my dear," he said in a purring, intimate voice, "that you dress like a whore?"

Sophie paled, then looked at Raider for assistance. He remained seated, holding perfectly still. Seeing that he had still not goaded Raider quite far enough, the German leaned further forward, his left arm braced on top of the table next to Sophie, while at the same time he reached down with his right, sliding his hand in between the deep valley of her breasts.

Sophie gasped, too frozen with shock to move. Raider took a moment to figure out what his best move would be; he couldn't let this go on.

The big Prussian looked somewhat off balance, but Raider knew that he had probably planned it to look that way. His right hand was really not all that far from the butt of his revolver, which clearly showed now, because the man's position had made his jacket gape open. One move from Raider and the German's hand would rise from Sophie's breasts and streak for the gun, while his companions went for theirs.

Raider knew that there was no longer any point in putting off the confrontation. They would continue to push until they had him in a corner. Besides, there was that hand on Sophie's breasts. Raider felt a red mist of rage flaring inside him, but managed to suppress it, knowing he'd need to keep his cool. Instead, he let the rage develop into an icy desire to wipe out the big, grinning ape leaning over his . . . well, his and the Duke's girl.

When Raider finally made his move it was not the one his opponent expected. Or perhaps the man had grown too involved with Sophie's breasts. His left hand was still braced on the tabletop, only a few inches from Raider's left hand. Sophie, her face crimson with anger and shame, was struggling to push the man's hand away from her breasts. The violence of her movements put him slightly off balance. For just a second or two it looked like it was going to be difficult for him to reach for that gun butt.

Seizing the opportunity, Raider simply grasped the man's left wrist, twisted his hand away from the tabletop, and then pulled down hard. With his weight braced too far forward, the Prussian lost the last of his balance and fell straight down, with Raider guiding the man's fall so that his face smashed against the solid oak of the table. There was a spray of blood and broken teeth. The German's legs went limp. Raider let him slump down onto the floor.

Raider was already standing up, reaching for his Remington as the attacker nearest him went for his own pistol. Then Raider realized that he could not fire; a family with two children was seated at a table directly behind his target. He might hit them. But the German gunman was close enough so that Raider, who had drawn with his usual impressive speed, had the time to step forward and smash the heavy barrel of his pistol against the German's face before he could completely free his pistol from its shoulder rig. Down he went.

That left one more—and he was directly behind Raider. Raider knew he'd probably never be able to turn in time to drop the man, but he'd have to try. Expecting a bullet to smash into him at any second, Raider spun around—just as the sound of a shot rang out.

Raider flinched, but nothing hit him. Then he saw why. The Duke was standing a couple of yards from the third attacker, his little .41 derringer in his right hand, smoke curling from the top barrel. The gunman was clasping his right shoulder, his gun hand hanging limply at his side, muzzle pointing straight down at the floor. "If you do not drop it," the Duke said calmly. "I will discharge the other barrel straight into your head."

The pistol dropped, and then Raider spun around again. He still had two hurt but potentially dangerous opponents behind him. He was barely in time. The man he'd hit in the face with his pistol was still down, but the first man, the one who'd mauled Sophie's breasts, was trying to struggle up onto his knees, his right hand once again reaching into his coat.

Raider stepped up close and placed the muzzle of his Remington against the side of the man's head. "Try it, ol' son, an' I'll blow your brains all over the sauerkraut."

He emphasized his threat by cocking the .44. The awful *snick* as the hammer ratcheted back into full-cock position sounded very loud in a room that had by now gone deathly still.

The man let his hand fall away from his coat. Raider quickly reached inside the coat and removed the man's revolver. It was a big Smith and Wesson .44 Russian. Raider thrust it into his own belt. Then he remembered what this man had done to Sophie. The Prussian was trying to stand up now, but Raider suddenly hooked a heel behind his foot and sent him sprawling. "I think you owe the lady an apology," he said coolly.

The man, trying to struggle up again, snarled something back at him in German. Raider didn't understand the words, but had no trouble understanding that they were not meant to be compliments. Using his foot again, he jerked one of the man's arms out to the side. The man had been on his hands and knees, so he fell back down onto his face, leaving a smear of blood on the floor. His face was a wreck, bleeding badly from where he had struck it against the tabletop.

Jamming the sole of his boot against the back of the man's neck, Raider ground his face into the floor. "You're gonna apologize one way or the other, you scar-faced bastard," he gritted out.

"Raider," the Duke cut in, "we have more trouble. Over by the door."

Still holding the man down, grinding his face even more brutally into the floor, Raider turned his head far enough so that he could see the door. What he saw he did not like. Von Bock and two other men were standing in the doorway.

Don't he ever run outta help? Raider wondered. Damn, here he was, half off balance, three mean-looking bastards maybe twenty feet away, a man who'd love to kill him thrashing around under his right foot, the man he'd rapped in the face with his pistol groaning and starting to get up, and the Duke with only one shot left in his belly gun—which wasn't much use against a target more than a few feet away anyhow. Suddenly the odds had changed back against them.

Von Bock and his two men, having sized up the situation, were striding rapidly forward, hands hovering near their coats. He's going to try it—he's going to do his best to end it right here, Raider realized. We're gonna have us a gunfight.

Then suddenly a loud voice called out from directly behind von Bock, "Hold it right there, fellas, or I'll blow you into little bitty pieces."

Von Bock and his two men spun to the side, so that Raider could see behind them, and to his immense relief he saw Doc and the sheriff he'd gone to find standing in the doorway, backed up by three deputies, all of whom were carrying shotguns. Those shotguns were cocked and leveled, pointing straight at von Bock and his men.

Von Bock accepted the inevitable. His right hand fell away from his coat. When his men were slow to do the same—damn fanatics, Raider thought—von Bock rapped out a sharp order in German. Only then did his men relax, their hands falling limply to their sides.

The sheriff sent one of his men around to disarm von Bock and his two companions. Raider continued to grind his man's face down into the floor, while pointing his .44 at the man who'd gotten up. That one wasn't in much shape to fight, anyhow; his face was streaming blood from where the barrel of Raider's pistol had hit him. He was obviously still dazed and barely able to remain on his feet. Nevertheless, Raider continued to cover him.

Then the sheriff and his men came over and completed disarming the Prussians. "Let him up," the sheriff said to Raider. Raider complied, but as soon as his foot was lifted from the downed man's neck, the Prussian sprang angrily to his feet, turning to face Raider and the sheriff, fists clenched, his face promising murder. "Careful," the sheriff said, aiming his pistol at the man's chest.

It did little good. The man took a half step toward Raider, obviously intent on attacking him, even if it meant his death. Then von Bock's voice cut in, sharp and commanding. "Manteufel!"

The man stopped as if he'd hit a wall. One final imploring look at von Bock, then he subsided.

"So," Raider said quietly. "The name's Manteufel, is it?"

"Yes," Manteufel hissed. "A name I think that you will have cause to regret ever hearing, peasant."

"Maybe. Maybe not."

Sophie suddenly stormed up and delivered a roundhouse slap to Manteufel's face that jerked his head halfway around. She rattled off a long string of German words that caused Manteufel's face to flush angrily. He started to say something in reply, but Sophie spat at him, then turned and marched away, her back rigid. "You don't do so well against women, neither," Raider chuckled.

Manteufel spun around and gave him a glare so filled with hatred that Raider began to feel rather sorry that he hadn't killed the man while he'd had the chance.

He became aware that von Bock and the sheriff were arguing loudly. "But I cannot be this man that you say I am," von Bock was insisting.

"Well, that's what they all say, sport," the sheriff drawled. "But you sure as hell fit the description. So do these nasty-lookin' buggers with you."

Doc, deadpan, filled Raider in. "The sheriff's been on the lookout for a gang that knocked over a bank over in Kansas. He thinks he's found them."

Despite von Bock's ever more vehement denials, the sheriff's deputies were marching him and his men toward the door. "We're just gonna have to hold you in the hoose-gow until we can get someone here from over Kansas way to identify you," the sheriff said, quite amiable now. He looked over his shoulder and grinned at Doc and Raider. The debt had been paid.

von Bock took the opportunity to spin around and face the two Pinkertons. Death he could have taken. But to be thrown into jail like a common thief . . .

Joined by Manteufel's hate-filled glare, directed especially at Raider, the look on von Bock's face boded no good for the two Pinkertons. They knew that they'd made dangerous enemies. "I kinda think I'd rather have a passel o' Comanches after my hide," Raider muttered to Doc.

"I know how you feel."

"Good work, anyhow. The sheriff didn't put up no fight?"

"No. He was glad to oblige. But he told me that he couldn't hold them for any longer than a week."

"Well then, we'd better speed up gettin' the train across, then hit the road."

"They'll catch up with us eventually."

"Yeah. But the next time we see 'em, I'm gonna cut loose first an' ask questions later. None o' this polite, city-style chitchat."

CHAPTER EIGHT

The next morning they took the ferry across the Mississippi. The Germans were appropriately impressed by the vast flood of brown water. So impressed that Raider wondered if the Duke was going to say that there was certainly nothing like this in Wittgenstein.

The ferry nosed its way forward carefully, avoiding snags and sandbars. "The channel changes all the time," Doc explained to the Duke. "The current is constantly altering the bottom, piling up sand in one place, washing it away in another. That's why the pilot is taking his time."

"It looks as if not everyone is as careful," the Duke replied dryly. He pointed to the moldering wreck of a large paddle-wheel steamboat poking half out of the water near the bank.

"Unfortunately, there's a lot of carelessness," Doc admitted.

"Damn stupidity," Raider said dourly. "And a lotta greed."

Seeing the puzzled looks on the faces of the Duke and the two women, Doc explained. "You see, the boat owners have races. Part of it is for the fun of it, but part of it is, as Raider says, greed. The faster they can make the trip either up- or downriver, the more passengers and freight they can carry. Therefore, they make more money. Some boats are very famous for their speed, but eventually the captains put too much pressure on the engines, and the boiler goes. You've never seen a disaster until you've seen a steam boiler blow up." Doc shuddered, remembering.

"Yep," Raider cut in. "Blows the guts right out of a boat. Then the wreck usually catches fire if it don't sink too fast. People drown, burn up, get blown to pieces."

As if to illustrate the conversation, a huge stern-wheeler hove into view, steaming at high speed down-channel. Clouds of black smoke poured from its twin smokestacks, very dark against the gleaming white woodwork. A muddy brown wave curled away from its blunt bow.

"My God, it's heading straight at us!" the Duke gasped.

Indeed it was. Growing steadily in size as it approached, the stern-wheeler showed no signs either of slowing or of altering its course. Neither did the ferry. Locked into their pride, neither captain wanted to give way to the other. The three Germans began to grow very nervous. So did the two Pinkertons, but they refused to let it show in front of foreigners.

Caught by the current, the ferry was slipping somewhat downstream despite the churning of its small side paddles. The big steamboat heading downriver drew closer and closer. Blasts of sound erupted from its whistle, warning the smaller boat out of the way, although the ferry had the right-of-way.

But right-of-way mattered not at all in the wide-open competition of the river. The ferry captain, rather pale now, stood determinedly on his bridge, glaring to his right at the approaching juggernaut, refusing to give in.

When it looked like an inevitable collision was about to occur, fate and the river lent a hand. A snag reared out of the water just in front of the ferry, with a sandbar behind it. Now the ferry captain had a face-saving excuse. He grabbed at it, spinning the wheel furiously. The little ferry swung to the left in a big arc, missing the snag and detouring around the sandbar—and incidentally moving out of the way of the approaching steamboat.

Everyone, including Doc and Raider, let out a sigh of relief as the big boat swept majestically by. It was so close, less than fifty yards away, that it was possible to make out

the features of the passengers who lined its rails, and to
realize that their faces were just as pale and strained as the
faces on the ferry. White knuckles still gripped the beauti-
fully polished railings. However, having survived, the passengers of the two boats waved gaily to each other.

"There are so many of them," Emma said. True enough,
it seemed that every foot of space on the other boat's deck
was crammed with humanity.

"They make more money that way," Raider said.

"Oh. I see."

By then the big stern-wheeler had passed by. There was
time for one last look at the intricate white gingerbread of
its woodwork, then a glance through the whirling paddle
wheel and up into its central lounge, where mobs of people
were seated at small tables, eating and drinking, with other
people going in and out of the small cabins on either side
of the lounge. The careless magnificence of the big boat
quickly dwindled in size as it sped on downriver, and now
the ferry was once again moving across-channel, heading
for the shore.

There was a carriage waiting at the dock for the Duke's
party, but they still had to shoulder their way through the
throng. Doc could see that the Germans were not used to
fending for themselves. It was easier to imagine them in
Europe, with police and troops forcing the crowds aside for
them, the people moving back deferentially, quite cowed.
None of that here. It was all raucous democracy, every man
equal, every man for himself.

There was an identical mob scene at the railroad yard.
The Duke's train sat off by itself, quite tranquil, but the
rest of the yard seethed with humanity, most of it rather
ragged. "Immigrant train," Raider said, pointing to a long
line of railway cars, minus an engine.

"What an awful-looking train," the Duke said, staring at
the ramshackle cars.

"Well," Raider said somewhat testily, "here in America
trains ain't just for the rich."

"Obviously not," the Duke answered.

He insisted on going closer. Looking in through the window of one of the cars, he studied the hard wooden benches that made up the seats. A curtained area at one end of the car comprised a crude and rather smelly toilet. A cast-iron stove was situated at the other end, although it was hardly needed at the moment; it was a hot and muggy day, and obviously stifling inside the car, which was packed with people, although many of its passengers were wandering around outside, getting what air they could. Without an engine, there wasn't much danger of the train departing without them.

"Why are they just sitting here?" Emma asked Doc, clearly appalled by what she saw.

"Well . . ." Doc started to say, but Raider cut in.

" 'Cause the damn railroad thieves are probably usin' the engine on a train that's more 'important.' Which means a train pullin' in more money."

"How awful," Emma said, watching with pity as a worn-looking woman tried to quiet several small, apparently hungry children.

"Not really," Doc said somewhat irritably. "For the most part these people are immigrants. Europe's poor. That's where they originally got in this condition, and I rather imagine that most of them are quite happy to be here, to have a chance to go out West, to have a chance to make something of themselves, which they would never be able to do in Europe. They're here for a reason: they're looking for homes, for land, for the opportunity to be something besides someone else's servant. And where else, how else, could they travel from one coast of a vast continent to the other coast for forty dollars apiece? Do you hear them complaining?"

Somewhat surprised by this bit of egalitarian sentiment that had burst, unbidden, from him, Doc fell silent. The Duke and Emma nodded thoughtfully. Sophie was looking rather interestedly at a rather handsome man on the far side of the train.

Suddenly the Duke turned and walked away. At first Doc thought he must be annoyed, perhaps insulted, by what he had said. But the Duke was walking with purpose, and Doc soon saw what the purpose was. The Duke entered a big general store on the far side of the station. Buttonholing a clerk, he began ordering large quantities of supplies. Within fifteen minutes a huge load of food, blankets and cooking utensils was being transported to the immigrant train, while the Duke counted over a thick wad of banknotes to the clerk.

As he led the way to his own train, the Duke appeared to be a little embarrassed. Emma took his arm. "It was worth doing," she said. "Who knows? Perhaps some of them were from Wittgenstein."

"Never!" the Duke burst out angrily. "Possibly some might be from countries which that monster, Bismarck, has enslaved, but not from Wittgenstein. No, I would never let my people sink to such a condition!"

Although Raider had been impressed by the Duke's generous action, he now permitted himself an internal sneer, suspecting that this was probably the first time His Royal Highness had been so close, physically, to the common man. Still, not too bad for a duke.

They boarded their train and were underway in half an hour. Everyone relaxed as the train steamed along, clickety-clacking over the rails. Von Bock was well behind them now, at least temporarily out of action. And half a continent lay ahead, most of it essentially empty, wild, virgin territory. The very act of passing through this vast land was in itself an adventure.

They headed northwest toward Nebraska. The route, the only rail route so far to cross the continent, would take them through Omaha, then on to Cheyenne, over the Continental Divide, then past Reno, over the Sierras, and finally down into California's huge Central Valley.

The transcontinental railroad had been completed only seven years before, as soon as the nation had recovered sufficiently from the terrible drain of the Civil War. It had been a vast undertaking, the most impressive engineering project of its day. Thousands had died blasting tunnels through mountains, pushing rails over swamp and prairie, fighting Indians and bandits, but the Pacific railroad was now a reality. A journey that had previously taken immigrants months in their covered wagons, crawling across the vast western plains only to face the final barrier of awesome mountains, or sailing around Cape Horn, or risking fever and bandits to make the shorter Panama crossing, had now been reduced to between five days and a week.

Raider and Doc had made the trip a number of times. Sometimes, when the case they were working on called for it, they'd suffered the rigors of the immigrant train. On other occasions, but not often, they had traveled first class.

Doc loved first class, he loved the luxury of the big Silver Palace cars with their gilt and red velvet and rich wooden paneling. He especially loved the service, particularly the excellent food, served on fine china by well-trained waiters, while the less fortunate passengers fought to bolt down a greasy meal at the infrequent twenty-minute food stops scheduled by the railroad. He appreciated the club cars, with their gambling tables, the organist working hard at his instrument, the well-dressed people, the comfortable Pullman sleeping cars, the entire ambience of slipping across the country in comfort and style.

Raider, on the other hand, hated it. He hated being surrounded by his class enemies, hated the waste, the pretensions, the stuffiness. Doc knew that Raider would probably just as soon ride his horse all the way across, given enough time.

The Duke and his two women took it all quite for granted. Seated comfortably in large easy chairs, drinking iced champagne—they had picked up a supply of ice in St.

Louis—or sipping fine wines, brandies, and liqueurs, they lazily watched the land slip away past the car's big windows.

The first day took them through Missouri. The Duke was not that interested in the landscape. They had clearly not reached the real West yet—there were too many farms, too much cleared land.

"This is where Jesse James came from," Doc told him. "He grew up on a hardscrabble little farm just like those out there."

"Really? How interesting. What a fascinating life he must have led."

"Unfortunately, he's still living it, and I doubt it's much of a life. He's simply a killer, and he started killing young. During the war, when he was still just a boy, he and his brother Frank rode with Quantrill's Raiders. They were a guerrilla band...more bandits, I suppose, than anything else. I suspect they were in it simply for the rape and plunder. For some reason, Jesse was called Dingus back in those days. Young Dingus was in on one of Quantrill's biggest raids, when they wiped out an entire town. Massacred the entire population—men, women and children. He hasn't stopped since."

"He tried for a while," Raider cut in. "After the war. But the damn Yankees wouldn't let him be. Now, don't get me wrong. I don't have no love for Jesse; he's a killer all right, but I kinda think I understand some of his feelin's."

Doc mulled that one over. Both he and Raider had been too young to actually fight in the Civil War, but they'd been old enough to witness its ravages and to pick up some of the hates and prejudices that the war and its aftermath had bred. Doc's sympathies were essentially Northern, while Raider's were Southern. Eleven years after its end, the war was still a volatile subject. It was not something the two of them could talk about without getting into violent, and sometimes bloody, arguments.

They both let the matter drop, each of them looking

glumly out the train window as the flat land moved by. The next day they were well into Nebraska, nearing Omaha.

"It's all so flat," the Duke said, staring off across the prairie. "How long has it been since we've seen a tree? It reminds me of the Russian steppes . . . of the Ukraine. I keep expecting to see Cossacks galloping past."

"Out here we call 'em Indians," Raider said.

Omaha did not entice them to disembark. The servants purchased a few supplies. There was no ice, so the champagne would have to wait until they could find some other way to keep it cold. Then they continued on.

The Duke and the women were clearly getting a little bored—until they sighted the buffalo herd. There were about two hundred of the big animals scattered over several acres, heads down, grazing.

"Damn! I didn't think there were still any down this far," Raider said excitedly.

"There used to be more?" Sophie asked. To her European eyes, the huge, black, humped backs poking up above the tall prairie grass seemed numerous enough. And somewhat threatening. They were so big.

Raider snorted. "Used to be millions. Why, when the first trains came through, it sometimes took them hours to pass just one herd."

Skeptical eyes turned toward him. His face darkened. "It's true, damn it! Then they started shootin' 'em, first for their fur, later for meat, both for the Army an' for the tame Indians. Did it myself, till I learned better. Shot meat for the Army. Yep, in the last ten years we've wiped out almost all of 'em. Wiped out one o' the things that made the West the West."

The Duke insisted that the train be stopped so that he could take a closer look at the buffalo. There was a considerable argument with the engineer. "Aren't no sidings to pull off on," he insisted stubbornly. But the Duke insisted just as stubbornly, and, after checking his schedules, the engineer decided that no trains were due for a while. "An hour," he said. "I'll give you an hour. No more."

Sophie was more annoyed than the Duke by this show of *lèse-majesté*. Not having status of her own, she was more prompt to fight for its outward appearance than the Duke was. Raider, annoyed, repaired to his and Doc's car. He sat by himself in the cool interior of the car, sipping a beer and mulling over how much trouble Sophie was becoming. Since they had crossed the Mississippi, she had tried to sneak into his bed on more than one occasion. Each time, aware of the close quarters in which they all lived, he'd sent her packing. She had lately taken to sulking when he was around, and he was worried that her behavior would alert the Duke.

Raider was pulled from his reveries by the sudden loud sound of a shot. Then there was another. He was already on his feet and running toward the Duke's car when a third shot sounded.

He found Doc sitting in the Duke's car, talking unconcernedly to Emma. The Duke was nowhere in sight. "Where the hell is he?" Raider demanded.

Doc made a face. "Really, Raider, you should try to do something about your language."

Raider fumed while a fourth shot banged out. He might have shouted at Doc again, but he could see now that something unusual was bothering his partner.

"He's back at the caboose," Doc finally said. "Shooting buffalo."

"What?" Without another word, Raider stalked angrily toward the rear of the train. Sure enough, the Duke was standing on the rear platform of the caboose, potting buffalo. Buffalo are quite stupid, and they had not yet connected the loud reports of the gunshots with the dead animals lying amongst them. Perhaps their dim little brains identified the sound as thunder. As it was, there were four down, and the Duke was reaching for another rifle. He had several stacked near at hand. His valet was taking each empty rifle from him, then presenting him with a reloaded one.

Raider felt the steam rising inside him. Necessary killing he could understand, but this was the same kind of slaughter that had destroyed the seemingly numberless buffalo herds.

The Duke caught sight of Raider. His face was flushed, his eyes glittering. "Wonderful shooting!" he said gaily, reaching for another rifle. This time it was the Winchester .44-40.

"Hey, wait!" Raider called out, but it was too late. The Duke had already fired his bullet into a huge bull standing about fifty yards away.

Up until now the Duke had been using the big Sharps rifles and the Ballard. Their heavy bullets had dropped the animals dead in their tracks, but now the lighter bullet from the Winchester simply drilled a hole in the big bull's side, far back on its body. Too far back, Raider realized, as he watched a puff of dust blossom from its thick hide. This was going to mean trouble. Gut-shot and hurting badly, the animal went crazy, spinning around in circles, bellowing, swiping at other bulls with its big horns and finally racing off clumsily over the prairie, away from the train.

All this sudden wild activity panicked the other animals. Tails up, heads down, they thundered off across the grassland in a compact black lump, heading in the general direction the wounded bull had taken. The Duke looked disappointed as he handed the Winchester back to his loader. "It was wonderful while it lasted," he said regretfully. "Well, at least we'll make the engineer happy. He can get the train moving now."

"Ain't you forgettin' somethin', Your Worship?" Raider asked in a dangerously calm voice.

The Duke's eyebrows rose. Raider seldom called him anything but "Duke."

"The buffalo," Raider prompted. "The one you

wounded. You just gonna leave it out there, gut-shot?"

The Duke scratched his chin. "I hadn't thought of that," he murmured, a little embarrassed, but also annoyed. He was not used to being talked to in such a manner by a man obviously his social inferior. "Oh well, I'm sure it'll die soon enough. You'd better tell the engineer to get the train moving."

"Uh-uh," Raider said flatly. "This train ain't movin' until we finish off that bull—even if I have to put a bullet through the engine boiler."

"Now see here, Raider..."

Doc had now come out onto the back of the caboose. "He's right, Your Highness. It's got to be done. We don't leave wounded animals to die. At least, not Raider and myself."

The Duke chewed his mustaches for a moment. He finally nodded. "All right. Shall we all go after him, then?"

"Ain't necessary," Raider replied. "Anyhow, we ain't got time to chase one wounded bull all over the prairie. Not without horses. I'll take him from here."

"But you can't mean that!" the Duke burst out. "Why, that animal must be a thousand yards away!"

"Yep."

Raider was already slipping a shell into the breach of one of the Sharps rifles. It was a big shell; it looked like a smallish milk bottle, capped by an enormous chunk of lead. He then picked up a pair of sticks that were lightly lashed together near one end, then jumped down onto the ground next to the caboose. "This is the way we did it when all the buffalo huntin' was goin' on," he said. "We'd take 'em on from about this distance. That way they didn't smell us, an' the sound o' the shot was too far away to bother 'em. We could drop maybe a hundred, two hundred animals 'fore they got the wind up."

"But the distance, man..."

"Yep. A longish shot," Raider admitted. "Longer'n normal."

He had shoved the sharpened bottom ends of the sticks into the soft soil, about a yard apart. Now the upper ends, above the lashings, formed a vee, a support. Raider sat down cross-legged on the ground, then laid the forearm of the rifle in the vee. Next, he raised the fold-up sight and set the crossbar at one thousand yards.

The Duke watched exasperatedly as Raider settled himself more securely, placed the butt of the rifle against his shoulder, then pulled back the big hammer. "You're wasting time with this ridiculous display," he snapped. "Let's go on out there and get it over with."

Doc said nothing. He knew better. Silence fell as Raider patiently sighted down the long barrel of the big Sharps, trying to fix the buffalo in the sights. It was a hot day, and the heat shimmer distorted the animal's black bulk. That far away, it looked tiny.

Raider blinked, and then everything cleared. The black-painted vee of the rear sight, the sharp blade of the front sight, the distant shape of the buffalo all came into focus. He held his breath, putting light pressure on the trigger. Each time his heart beat, the rifle's front sight jumped a little. Silent, unmoving, he only put pressure on the trigger between heart beats.

As should happen when a shot is correctly executed, it was a surprise to Raider himself when the rifle finally went off. He had been so relaxed, so lost in concentration, that the heavy recoil slammed him backwards, lifting his feet off the ground.

The others jumped too, startled by the loudness of the report. Doc was sure that he caught a momentary glimpse of the bullet as it soared toward the target in a high parabolic arc. After a seeming eternity, during which nothing more seemed to happen, the Duke began to swear. Then the buffalo suddenly disappeared, dropping straight down as the massive bullet tore through its heart. It was dead before it hit the ground.

The Duke was stunned. He stood openmouthed. "I don't believe it," he muttered.

Raider stood up. "Believe it or not, how about gettin' cookie and some helpers down on the ground to cut up these here buffalo. You ain't lived till you ate buffalo hump. The tongue's good too."

The Duke continued to shake his head. "I still don't believe it," he repeated.

Raider grinned. "Oh, it wasn't all that hard; there was hardly any wind. An' besides, the buffalo wasn't shootin' back."

CHAPTER NINE

The engineer was growing frantic by the time Raider was satisfied that they had done all they could with the mountains of buffalo meat lying slaughtered on the prairie grass. He'd only bothered with the four animals the Duke had dropped near the train. The other one, the one he'd dropped with the Sharps, was too far away; he'd end up as a gift for the crows and coyotes.

Raider had made sure that the big animals were skinned as well as cut up for meat. The hides now resided in the baggage car, along with the immense head of one of the bigger bulls. "We'll drop it off in Cheyenne," Raider told the Duke. "We'll get it mounted, an' you can stick it on the wall of your castle."

By the time the train got moving again it was quite a bit later than the engineer had intended. There was a fast passenger train scheduled to pass them soon, heading west, and a slow freight coming the other way. The engineer poured on the coal, pushing the train hard. For a while they were bowling along at a blistering, train-rattling fifty miles an hour.

The engineer found the siding he'd been looking for just in time. The eastbound freight was already on it; there was barely room to squeeze in the Duke's train. Ten minutes later the westbound express roared by, its passengers waving gaily at the Duke's train. Human beings were few and far between out on this vast prairie.

While the train was parked on the siding, the cook prepared a vast amount of buffalo meat. At first the women refused to eat any of it; their minds were full of images of the big, shaggy, smelly animals lying dead on the ground. But after some coaxing, first Emma, then Sophie tried timid mouthfuls—and soon were begging for more. By then the Duke had already finished his first steak and was sampling the fatty hump meat that the cook had piled up on a platter in the middle of the table.

They all ate until they could eat no more, Doc and Raider matching the Germans bite for bite. Leaning back, stifling a belch, while the Duke belched unembarrassedly, Doc reflected that this was the first time he'd ever eaten buffalo hump at a table. He'd always connected buffalo meat with life on the trail: a cold camp, eating on the hard ground with grit in the meat and ants fighting him for his meal, the buffalo half raw. But now, here he was, reaching for one last piece of tender, perfectly prepared buffalo tongue, roasted in garlic sauce, while seated at a big walnut table covered with a damask tablecloth, eating his buffalo off fine china, using heavy silver cutlery, and washing the meat down with an excellent claret. The Duke certainly had a genius for making life on the trail comfortable.

The train crew had also been fed as much of the meat as they could hold. Now, bloated, they got the train underway, backing it off the siding away from the freight, then pulling out onto the main track to head west once again.

The problem was, what were they going to do with the rest of the meat? They had far more than they'd be able to eat before it began to go bad; the weather was very hot. "Too bad there ain't no Injuns around," Raider said. "They sure could use it."

Later that afternoon Raider spotted a low shape a couple of hundred yards from the track. "Hey, Duke, can you stop the train?" he called out.

As usual, Doc winced at his partner's style of courtly address, but the Duke obligingly reached up and tugged on the emergency stop cord. By now the engineer knew that a tug on the cord was less likely to signal an emergency than a ducal whim. The train slowed to a smooth stop.

A few minutes later the engineer was in the car. "What is it this time?" he asked grumpily.

"How long till the next train?" Raider asked.

"Not for hours. What the hell you got up your sleeve?"

"I saw a house out there. Maybe we can get rid o' some o' the meat.

"House? I don't see anything," the Duke said, peering out over the prairie.

"Out there," Doc said, pointing.

It was very hard to see, just a slight break in the smooth, slightly rolling contour of the prairie. The fact that it was more or less the same color as the land didn't help.

"A soddie," Doc explained. "A sod house. Made out of turf."

Gradually everyone was able to make out the house's shape, and then the shapes of people standing beside it—a woman, and smaller figures that had to be children.

"Let's go take a look," Raider said, jumping down from the train.

By the time they got to the soddie, a man was galloping an old plow horse in their direction from behind a small rise. He had an ancient muzzle-loading rifle clutched in one hand. The horse was laboring but coming on fast.

Doc and the Duke were not far behind Raider. He signaled for them to hold still, then raised his right hand in a gesture of greeting and friendship, then walked forward to meet the horseman.

Farmer, rather. He was a medium-sized man, dressed in ragged work clothes and dusty high-top shoes. He had bright blue eyes and a big bushy mustache. Raider estimated his age at about thirty. He slid down from the horse and waited as Raider approached. Raider noticed that the old rifle was more or less pointing in his direction. "Afternoon," he said amiably.

"Aftairnoon," the man replied in a heavily accented voice.

"We have some buffalo meat on the train. More'n we can use," Raider continued. "Maybe you an' your family might—"

The man's eyes lit up. *"Sacre bleu!"* he burst out. Turning toward the soddie, he shouted, "Marie!" following the name with a gargle of thick French. French-Canadian, Raider realized.

A worn-looking woman came out of the soddie. At first glanced Raider estimated her age at perhaps forty. Maybe she was the farmer's older sister, or his aunt. Then he took a closer look and decided that, under her frontier exhaustion, the woman might only be in her late twenties. Behind her, a gaggle of children moved shyly out into the open, the youngest perhaps one year old, the oldest about nine. The thin wail of a baby's crying sounded from inside the soddie. No wonder she looks all tuckered out, Raider thought.

They began moving the meat at once. The French-Canadian—Pierre, his name was—hitched a rickety wagon to his swaybacked nag and drove over to the train. While the men were loading meat, Sophie and Emma disembarked, attracted by the children. Dressed in tattered clothing, big-eyed, and for the most part snot-nosed, the children gazed, fascinated, at these elegant, well-dressed beings from another, faraway world.

Sophie easily made friends with some of the smallest; her cheerful manner soon had them laughing and prancing about her. The wife, Marie, held back shyly, obviously embarrassed by the shabbiness of her clothing. It was Emma who eventually put her at her ease, and soon the two women were talking, Marie desperately, as if she had been dying of hunger for conversation. It was not an easy conversation; only Pierre spoke any English, and the family's French was amazingly thick French-Canadian patois that was very difficult for the Europeans to understand.

The Duke insisted that they all share some of the train's bounty. Wine was brought to the house, and sweets for the children. Emma, who was more or less the same size as Marie, had three of her older dresses brought from the train. After a great deal of insisting on Emma's part, Marie finally accepted them, with tears in her eyes.

Pierre, lubricated by the wine, became very talkative. "We are here only one year," he told the Duke and the two Pinkertons. "We 'ave in Canada big plantation . . . 'ow you say? Farm? We 'ave big 'ouse, lots of land. My family is there evair since the French Revolution. We do ver' well, we are per'aps even rich. Then the British come. They attack the house in the night, burn it down. They kill two of the smallest children, but the rest of us, we get away into the woods. Thair is nothing left, an' we know they will kill us if we try to come back. They want our land. So we come down 'ere, several families of us. We come to this 'ard place."

The Duke, who had several English cousins, including members of the Royal Family, was somewhat disturbed by this story, but hardly surprised. He knew the British. There was really nothing he could say, so he didn't.

Soon it was time to go. The engineer was blasting frantically on the train's whistle. The Duke and his party stood up, taking one last look at the soddie. It was made up of blocks of turf cut out of the grassy soil and stacked up like bricks over a deep rectangle that had been dug into the ground. It was not very pretty, and insects tended to remain in the sod, but it was warm in the winter, which was horribly cold, and cool in the summer. Its low profile also gave it protection against tornadoes.

Goodbyes were said in front of the house. Pierre proudly paraded his many offspring, most of whom had not yet been introduced to the men. "This is Guy, and this is Ernie, and this is Albina, and Ollie, and this is little Marie-Louise."

Marie-Louise was Emma and Sophie's favorite. She was a tiny little two-year-old with a serious and dignified demeanor. Her two older sisters held her hands protectively while Emma kissed her on the forehead. The little girl's huge eyes remained fixed on the two women as they turned and walked toward the train.

Pierre accompanied the men back to the train. "There is a lot of meat," he said. "But we will cure some of it, make pemmican. An' what we cannot use, we will give to our neighbors."

Neighbors? The land seemed deserted, but perhaps, ten miles away, there were other hardscrabble dirt farmers. "I suspect that it is a hard life you live," the Duke said.

Pierre's face darkened. *"Oui.* The prairie, she does not forgive if you make a mistake. She kills you. Kills the children especially . . . and the women."

He looked enviously over the track. "I 'ave 'eard much about California. Per'aps someday. . ."

The Duke's party boarded the train and were soon underway, the Duke and the women standing on the back platform of their car, waving to the small figures standing so forlornly by their primitive dwelling, until they had disappeared into the gathering dusk. As they went back into the car, the Duke ruminated on the immigrant trains. "Is this what they are heading toward?" he asked the two Pinkertons.

Raider shook his head. "Not all of 'em. That bunch just didn't go far enough west."

It was a day later, when they were nearing Cheyenne, that they saw their first Indians. Raider heard Sophie call out in alarm, and a moment later the Duke's voice boomed excitedly. Raider ran to where they were peering out of a window. Bending down, he saw four mounted Indians riding along about a hundred yards from the train. "Omahas," he said curtly.

"Are they dangerous?" Sophie asked, breathless with excitement.

Raider took a longer look at the Indians. They had ridden in closer to the train, close enough so that he could see that they were wearing mismatched bits and pieces of cast-off white-man's clothing. One had a flattened and filthy top hat on his head, with his braids hanging down behind. Two carried rifles, battered but probably serviceable. The stocks were decorated with nail heads and bits of fluttering cloth. One was fairly new, a Winchester '66 lever-action repeater.

The only part of their equipment that was in really good shape was their horses. Fattened on the prairie grass, the animals were sleek and well-muscled. Yipping, the Indians suddenly spurred the animals into a run, swerving in toward the train. Raider's hand automatically reached out for a rifle, which terrified the women. Then he let his hand drop down toward his side. "They just want to race us. Just have a little fun."

"They're not dangerous, then?" the Duke asked.

"Well, I wouldn't want to have 'em come up on my camp in the dark. Just the fact that they're out there . . . Well, you see, the Army's cleared just about all the Indians outta these parts. Didn't want 'em botherin' the settlers, askin' for their land back. Those bucks out there are off their reservation. Slipped away. Which means they may be out for trouble as much as for fun. But four Injuns with two rifles ain't about to attack a train."

Sure enough, the riders soon peeled off to the side, whooping, dwindling into small black dots as the train moved away. Everyone on the train was thinking about the French-Canadian family, alone back there on the prairie, but they were at least eighty miles back, hopefully out of harm's way.

They pulled into Cheyenne later that day. It had been agreed that here they would split up. The Duke and Raider would head north, toward the Dakotas and the last of the big game herds. The women would stay on the train with Doc, heading south to Denver.

There had been a great deal of argument. "We should stay together," Doc had insisted. "Von Bock's going to be on our trail soon enough. With you and the Duke on your own, with no help in sight . . ."

It was the Duke who'd made the final decision. He had come to the New World to hunt, and hunt he would. There was, of course, no question of taking the women with them; Raider had explained the wildness of the land they would be passing through. Anyhow, it was not that long a run to Denver, a little more than a day on the train. Emma and Sophie would be safe there.

Cheyenne was the real West, a small but busy frontier station, full of prospectors, hunters, gamblers, farmers, and soldiers. To the north there was nothing but Indian country, with many tribes still inhabiting their ancestral range, despite the Army's earnest attempts to either exterminate them or round them up and ship them south to land no white man as yet wanted. Which was pretty much the same as exterminating them, since nothing but rattlesnakes and rabbits had much chance of making a living off the barren southern reservations.

In Cheyenne, Raider bought horses and trail supplies and hired two half-breeds to help with the skinning and the camp work. During this time, the train remained on a siding close to the little station. Everyone was still living aboard, since there were no accommodations in town to equal it in either luxury or security. The Duke enjoyed a last couple of days of good wine and rich food, along with a soft bed full of Sophie—much to Raider's annoyance— and then they were ready to ride.

There was a last farewell, Doc still upset about splitting up the party, the Duke alive with excitement, Emma regal, Sophie wiping an eye—for two men of course, but Raider hoped that the Duke still didn't know that. And then they were off, riding out of the little frontier post into the vast grasslands, heading north toward adventure.

CHAPTER TEN

Once they had left the town behind them, Raider immediately felt much more at ease. The plains stretched away to the horizon, with not a building, not a road, not a person in sight. There was only this one small group, lost in the immensity of it all, riding toward the far north.

That night they made camp twenty miles north of Cheyenne. Lying in his bedroll, Raider stared up at the stars. At this time of year the weather was very clear. The Milky Way stretched overhead in a luminescent arc. It was so goddamn beautiful it made a man ache.

A wolf howled in the distance. The only other sounds were the slight soughing of the wind, an occasional snort or stamp from the horses, and the even breathing of the men.

"Duke?" Raider called out softly.

"Yes?" The Duke wasn't asleep yet either.

"You like it out here?"

A moment's silence. "Yes."

"Anything like this in Wittgenstein?"

A chuckle from the Duke. "No. But there are other things there."

"Yeah, I s'pose so. It's home, ain't it."

Another pause. "Yes . . . home."

The next morning the Duke shot two antelope. Raider had the two half-breeds skin and butcher them. The hides and the horns went onto a packhorse. The animal bucked at first, offended by the blood smell, but soon quieted down.

All of the horses would eventually grow used to the smell of blood.

They moved steadily north, doing a little shooting now and then, but mainly just admiring the land. It was easy to become disoriented in this kind of terrain. The plains were so vast that it seemed they weren't making any progress at all but rather walking in place, with the same horizon, the same sky, constantly before them.

On the fourth day they arrived at Fort Laramie. It was not a prepossessing place, just a log stockade built at the confluence of the Platte and the North Platte rivers. "The usual fort. Army inside, Injuns outside," Raider commented to the Duke as they neared the fort. Sure enough, the Stars and Stripes flew over the stockade, while outside were gathered a ragtag collection of tepees and brush shelters. "Treaty Injuns," Raider told the Duke. "Lookin' for somethin' to eat."

"They don't have any food of their own?"

"Used to. The buffalo. They lived off 'em. Ate the meat, used the hides to make tepees an' sleepin' robes, used the bones for tools an' needles, the sinews for thread —hell, they didn't waste a thing. Now they ain't got nothin'. No buffalo left around these parts. The last o' the herds are way up in the Dakotas, near the Canadian border."

The Duke felt a twinge of shame over his careless buffalo slaughter near Omaha. He wished he had the meat now to give to these people. They certainly looked as if they could use it. Hunger was very evident, not only in the thin bodies but most of all in the eyes. It was the look of hopelessness on the faces of the children that most bothered the Duke. "Doesn't your government do anything about this?" he demanded, conveniently forgetting the starving millions in Europe's slums.

"Sure. It sends out troops to kill 'em," Raider snapped. He was more bothered than he cared to admit. These were Arapahos. He remembered the Arapaho as bold, fierce warriors, proud riders. These miserable refugees, mostly women and children and old men, were a travesty of the fiercely independent people he remembered. The few younger men were mostly afoot, and without weapons. They wouldn't be able to kill a buffalo if it jumped up in front of them. He hated the sight of them dressed in ridiculously mismatched pieces of white man's clothing. It was the damned farmers, he thought bitterly. Eatin' up all the land, with their soddies and their fences and their raggedy families and their worn-out wives.

They bypassed the fort; Raider was in no mood to talk to soldiers. They made camp for the night several miles from the fort, and for the first time Raider posted a night guard.

"Are you expecting trouble?" the Duke asked.

Raider shrugged. "Nothin' in particular. But if you was one o' them hungry Injuns, wouldn't you maybe kinda like to have our guns an' our horses an' our grub?"

Their route now began to angle slightly to the east. A range of hills lay ahead and to the right. After all this time passing over the prairie, first by train and now by horseback, to see those hills rising up out of the earth was quite startling.

"Those are the Black Hills," Raider said. "They're part of the Dakota Territory now, but most of the land around these parts is still Indian country. Sioux an' Cheyenne. From now on, keep your eyes peeled. The Cheyenne have been pretty well whipped by the Army, but not the Sioux. They're still runnin' around free as God made 'em."

"I'd like to go into the mountains," the Duke said.

Raider chewed his lower lip. "So would I. But maybe it ain't worth the risk. The Black Hills are Sioux country. To them it's sacred ground, an' they take that kinda thing pretty serious. They don't think too kindly of white men ramblin' around their sacred places. Not that the Army would let a little thing like that stop them from goin' on in."

"You sound like you don't like the Army."

"Not much."

The next day, when they were only a few miles from the lower slopes of the mountains, looking up wistfully at the cool, tree-clad heights, they ran smack into the Army. Raider saw them first, a long line of horsemen, wagons, and guns, strung out for more than a mile over the flat terrain. The Duke might not have noticed them had not the two breeds spotted the soldiers and set up a buzz of excited conversation.

Both Raider and the Duke pulled out field glasses and studied the soldiers. "One hell of a lot of 'em," Raider commented. "Maybe we can go around and avoid . . . Nope . . . they spotted us."

Through his glasses he watched a burst of activity around a knot of horsemen at the head of the column. Focusing more closely, he saw that one officer was looking back at him through another pair of field glasses. The distance was still too great for him to make out features, but he was pretty sure that the officer had long blond hair. "Damn," he muttered.

Unless Raider decided to change the direction the Duke's party was traveling in, their path would soon intersect the Army column's path. He had little doubt that, if he altered direction, the officer leading the column would send out troopers to see who he was, so he accepted the inevitable and guided his group on at a slow walk toward the soldiers.

The Duke seemed a little puzzled by Raider's behavior. "Do you have some special reason to be wary of soldiers?" he asked.

"Not no more'n any sensible man."

"But certainly, soldiers of your own country, detailed to protect the white man . . ."

"Yeah, sure, there's some good soldiers an' there's some fine officers leadin' 'em. But we don't happen to be headin' toward one o' them fine officers. Unless my eyes are gettin' old, that long-haired bastard out in front is none other than Colonel George Armstrong Custer."

A look of intense interest passed over the Duke's features. "The famous young general of your Civil War? The one they called 'The Boy General of the West'?"

"Yep. The very same one."

"Well, I'd feel honored to meet him."

"Yeah, an' I'm sure he'll feel that you *should* be honored."

"I take it that you don't quite approve of General Custer."

"Nope. An' it's Colonel Custer now, That must really kill him, to be only a colonel. He liked bein' a general. Bustin' his gut to become one again."

There wasn't much more time for talking; they were nearing the cavalry column. As it was, Raider fell into a glum silence from which the Duke's questions could not rouse him.

Riders dashed out from the column to shepherd them in. The column had stopped, and now Raider could see for certain that it was indeed Custer waiting for him. He had to admit that Custer was a handsome bastard. With his long yellow locks and neat mustaches, he looked like every boy's dream of a dashing cavalry officer.

Custer had been conversing with one of his officers, but now that the newcomers were approaching, he looked up. At first his face held an expression of polite but hauty interest. Then he suddenly scowled. "Raider!" he burst out. "Hasn't anybody hung you yet?"

"Not so's I'd noticed," Raider replied. "How about you?"

Custer's frown deepened. "I could probably have had you shot that time, you know."

"Naw, I don't think so."

"You disobeyed a direct order."

"I don't fight women an' kids."

"They were Indians, Raider. Hostiles."

"I don't fight hostile women an' kids either."

Custer had by now seen the Duke, who stood out very sharply against the backdrop of the two half-breeds. "Oh, yeah," Raider said. "This here's the Grand Duke o' Wittgenstein. In case you're wonderin', we're up here huntin'. The Duke likes to hunt."

Custer had heard little past the words "Grand Duke of Wittgenstein." He instantly rode closer. "Glad to make your acquaintance, Your Highness," he said, snapping a brief but sharp salute toward the Duke.

"And delighted to make yours," the Duke replied, reaching out and shaking Custer's hand. "Even all the way over in Europe, we have heard about the gallant General Custer."

Custer cast a furtive glance at the colonel's eagles on his shoulders, but chose for the moment to ignore them. Then he glanced over at Raider. "Don't you think it's a little risky bringing His Highness up into these parts with such a small escort?"

"Risky? Not that I'd heard. Why? Expectin' trouble from the Indians?"

"Possibly. There has been some raiding."

"Yeah. Ever since you shoved your way into the Black Hills in '74."

Custer glared at Raider, but instead of replying he turned back toward the Duke. "Perhaps you would like to accompany us, Your Highness. We're off on a small punitive expedition against the Sioux. I hear there's a large concentration of them over by the Little Big Horn River."

The Duke looked decidedly interested, but Raider refused bluntly. Custer tried to stare him down. Neither man would look away. "I could order you to go," he told Raider. "I could press you into duty as a scout."

"Yeah. An' when word got back to the State Department that you'd hauled a foreign duke into a fight, you'd end up bein' a captain."

A spasm of rage passed over Custer's face, but he

quickly brought himself under control. "All right, Raider, have it your way."

He wheeled his horse around and snapped an order to a captain, who snapped it on to a lieutenant, who passed it to a sergeant, who bellowed a command, and suddenly the column was in motion again, guidons flapping in the light breeze, equipment clanking, men turning to look at Raider and the Duke as they passed on by.

The Duke seemed thoroughly annoyed when he finally looked over at Raider. "Really, you might have consulted me first before you turned down the general's invitation. It's not every day—"

"Oh yeah? An' do you really like seein' people shot down, sabered, run over by horses?" Raider snapped back. "Do you like seein' dead women an' kids?"

"I'm certain that a fine officer like Custer would never—"

"He couldn't help it if he tried. The warriors live with their families. Did you see those two field guns? Round shot and canister don't pick out who's a warrior an' who's a woman or kid. Besides, this here's the Sioux peoples' homeland. Custer ain't got no right pushin' his way in there. I know for a fact that he's been ordered not to. But that ain't gonna make no difference to old Goldilocks. There might be a newspaper story in it. He might get more famous."

The Duke's expression changed to one of curiosity. "Do you really think that the general would exceed his orders?"

"Colonel," Raider corrected. "He's just a colonel. And yeah, you bet your ass he'd exceed his orders. He exceeded 'em two years ago when he first went into the Black Hills. That really riled up the Indians. He might of got into a lotta trouble over that, but then some bastard with him discovered gold up there. Now all of a sudden the land's worth a fortune an' white men are flockin' in like goddamn ants. Hell, nothin'll keep a white man out of a place if he smells gold, not all the Indians in the world. So now one o' the last places the red man had for himself is gonna be taken away from him. But it's gonna be bloody, 'cause the Sioux ain't gonna go down without a helluva fight."

The last of the cavalry column passed on by, the sound of the horses' hooves diminishing to a low pounding. A broad swath of grass had been pressed down, and probably would not rise again before the next year. It was midsummer, and hot and dry. The grass was a beautiful golden-yellow, and dry as tinder.

Raider got his little group moving again, still heading north. He called a stop after another mile or two. "I don't know if we should keep goin' on," he told the Duke.

"But why not?"

"There could be trouble. Custer's bustin' for a fight, an' he's headin' right into the middle of Indian country. I know the layout up there. It's a bad place for cavalry, good for Indians."

"Do you really think so? The terrain is that poor?

"Yeah. Lotsa places for the Sioux to hide. They're slippery bastards. It wouldn't surprise me none if Custer ended up gettin' his tail caught in a mighty big crack."

CHAPTER ELEVEN

As they continued north, Raider was uneasy. He told himself that it was because of the possibility of Custer riling up the Indians again, but that answer didn't totally satisfy him. He kept feeling an itching in his back, right between the shoulder blades—as if someone was behind him.

He finally decided to act on this feeling. Their present route was taking them along the western flank of the Black Hills. The ground was much more broken here, giving better cover, so, after sending the others on ahead, Raider rode up a small gully toward the mountains.

When he had found a good place of concealment that was high enough to overlook their back trail, he dismounted, then climbed up the sides of the gully and lay down under a bush. For the next ten minutes he studied the land to the south through his field glasses, slowly panning them from side to side, careful that the sun not shine on the lenses and thus give his position away.

There. About a mile back. A group of horsemen. They were passing under a screen of trees, so he couldn't quite see who they were. He couldn't even tell if they were white men or Indians.

Then they rode out into the open, and now he saw who they were: Von Bock with six men.

Damn! How had they gotten onto his trail? Then looking more closely, Raider saw that one of the men was an Indian. Smart move. Von Bock had hired an Indian tracker. Two of the other men looked like local gunfighter types.

The other three seemed to be part of von Bock's endless flock of Prussians.

Raider's first instinct was to set up an ambush and pick them off, but that was a dangerous, even foolhardy maneuver for one lone man against seven, and he didn't want to involve the Duke. Nor could he rely on his two half-breeds. They hadn't been hired on as gunfighters. No, the best thing would be to run like hell.

Fortunately, von Bock and company were stopping to rest their horses. Even at this distance Raider could see that the animals appeared to have been ridden very hard. They looked all done in. That was one break for his side, because he and the Duke had been very easy on their mounts; they were still in excellent condition.

Riding as quickly as he could without making either a lot of noise or a lot of dust, Raider caught up with the Duke and the two breeds within half an hour. He instantly dismounted and began transferring his saddle and bridle to a fresh horse. "You change mounts too," he told the Duke. "We got trouble."

"Indians."

"Nope. Von Bock. With a small army. We gotta make tracks."

A spasm of anger momentarily distorted the Duke's features. For a second Raider was afraid that he would insist on riding back and confronting von Bock. Fortunately he didn't, and in another five minutes they were all riding hard, still heading north, pushing their horses faster than Raider liked to push them. But he had a definite reason for getting as much out in front of their pursuers as possible.

"Where are we going?" the Duke asked after they had been riding about an hour.

"Up into the Black Hills. Then over toward Deadwood. It's the only real settlement around these parts. We can probably get help from the law—if there's any there."

The Duke actually began to look pleased. He had said

all along that he wanted to go into the mountains. "Why are we still riding north, then?" the Duke asked, looking over at the foothills, still to their right.

"I'm lookin' for a particular pass."

The Duke was less than pleased when Raider finally cut northeast. The pass he'd had in mind was narrow and strewn with fallen rock and other debris. "Lotta flash floods here in the spring and fall," Raider explained as the horses picked their way around boulders, dead tree limbs, and dried-out, uprooted bushes. The ground underfoot was mostly sand and sloped upward sharply, climbing higher into the hills. It was easy to imagine a wall of water raging down this big draw, carrying everything before it. Of course, there was no danger of that now; it was the middle of the dry season, and it hadn't rained for a long time. Nor would it rain again until late fall.

The going got more and more difficult as the draw got narrower and steeper. The two breeds, who had not been told the reason for this sudden change in the manner of their travel, were growing very nervous. It wasn't hard to deduce that Raider and the Duke were running from something rather than toward something. The two men began to hang back, muttering between themselves. "Come on, get your asses movin'," Raider snarled. "Hang back an' you'll get them asses shot off."

The breeds grew a littler more interested in speed, but Raider wondered how long they could keep it up. There weren't enough spare horses to allow for as many changes for the breeds as for himself and the Duke. He wasn't being callous. He knew that von Bock had no reason to harm the half-breeds.

Finally the draw got so narrow that they had to ride single file. The two breeds rode at the head of the file, pulling the pack animals after them, then came the Duke, then the spare mounts, which Raider did not want the breeds to have access to, and then Raider himself, keeping a sharp eye on the trail behind him.

He suddenly reined in his horse. "Wait! Hold up! This is the place!"

"For what?" the Duke called back. "Certainly you don't intend to make a stand here, man."

It was hardly a place for defense. The gully had by now turned into a steep gorge. Sheer walls sloped hundreds of feet above them. There was no cover at all, other than some smallish boulders, and the route ahead, the only possible escape route, was bare earth.

"Nope. We ain't gonna make a stand. But the chase ends here. Hold my horse, will you, Duke?"

Raider slipped down from the saddle. Fumbling in his saddlebags, he pulled out a pair of moccasins. While he sat down and pulled off his boots, he explained his plan to the Duke. "See those big boulders up above the trail, back there about fifty yards?" he said, pointing back down the gorge. Sure enough, several huge boulders hung above the trail. Teetered there, actually. It looked to the Duke as if nothing but wishful thinking was holding them in place. He shivered, happy they had not come tumbling down while he and the others were passing underneath.

"It was a real risk comin' up this way," Raider said as he pulled the soft moccasins onto his feet. "Last time I came through here, maybe two years ago, those rocks were already lookin' like they wanted to go. If they had, well, we'd be trapped the other side of 'em right now, with von Bock and his boys comin' up fast behind us."

"You took that chance?"

"Yeah. It seemed like it was worth it. Now I gotta get up there. See the path?"

A tiny trail, probably made by small animals, led up the side of the gorge. "Never would be able to make it with boots on," Raider said.

"You're not going to try going up there, Raider!" the Duke responded, aghast. "Why, only a goat—"

"*Ba-a-a-a-a,*" Raider replied, mimicking a goat's bleat.

Then he was off, first making a running start at the path, which took him up about ten feet. After that he had to dig in with his hands and toes, grabbing at anything that would help him assent.

His progress was slow. Small stones and bits of earth slid down behind him. It took him over half an hour to make it to a place right behind the huge, teetering boulders. Here he could rest a little; there was a small shelf behind the boulders where earth, washing down from the heights, had been trapped.

A small tree grew out of the shelf. Drawing his bowie, Raider hacked loose a branch about ten feet long and three inches thick. He stuck one end of it underneath the biggest of the boulders, then heaved hard, trying to dislodge it.

Nothing happened. Raider strained some more, his face darkening with the effort. Still nothing. "You'd better start riding," he called down to the Duke. "Just in case this don't work."

"No. I'm staying here."

The two breeds were already pushing their horses farther up the gorge. Raider positioned the branch once more. Another gasping heave, this time rewarded by a faint scraping sound.

Encouraged, Raider repositioned the lever and heaved again. There was a much louder grating sound, and the boulder moved a little. One more desperate heave and the boulder overbalanced. It hung for a moment, then slowly toppled over.

It was situated several yards above other boulders. On its way down, it dislodged those below. Suddenly, tons of rock were thundering down the sides of the gorge, piling up at the bottom.

The ground began to slip from beneath Raider's feet. He let go of the branch and grasped at the tree he had cut it from. For a moment it seemed as if the tree would go too, but the roots held.

A vast cloud of dust now obscured the floor of the gorge

below, but Raider could see mounds of rock thrusting up
out of the dust toward him. Just in time, because suddenly
he saw movement farther down the gorge. Damn! it was
two of von Bock's men, riding up fast. One look at their
lathered mounts told Raider that the animals had been
pushed near to death. He had no rifle with him, only his
pistol, but he drew it now and emptied the cylinder down
the gorge, firing more for the noise then for effect. The
range was too great for really accurate shooting.

The bullets caromed off the gorge walls, whizzing by
the pursuers. They instinctively threw themselves off their
horses and dove for cover behind some fallen debris.
Raider quickly reloaded and emptied another cylinder,
peppering the rocks the men were hiding behind. They
were firing back now.

Raider shoved the empty pistol back into its holster,
making sure that he slipped the leather thong that held the
pistol in place over the hammer. Then he quickly slid down
into the gorge. It was much easier going down than it had
been going up, because the rockfall had formed an incline.
It was still hard going, but Raider went full tilt, grabbing at
rocks, skinning his hands, descending with tremendous
speed.

When he reached the bottom, he picked up his boots
and leaped into the saddle. "Come on, let's get the hell out
of gun range."

The rockfall behind them would not, of course, stop a
man from climbing over it. But there was no way von
Bock was going to move horses around an obstacle like
that. On foot, he and his men would never catch up with
mounted men. For the time being, the chase was over.

CHAPTER TWELVE

The gorge finally opened out onto a small plateau surrounded by low, eroded hills. Although still fairly dry, these highlands were much more lush than the plains below. It was a quiet, beautiful, magical landscape. Raider had never had any trouble understanding why the Sioux considered it sacred. A sense of power emanated from this land. A sense of communion.

A few hours later they spotted Indians, Sioux warriors, half a dozen of them, riding single file across a meadow. Fortunately, the warriors did not see them. Raider concealed his party behind a low ridge until the Indians had ridden out of sight. "They sure don't look nothin' like those poor bastards we saw outside Fort Laramie, do they?" Raider whispered to the Duke.

The Duke studied the Indians through his field glasses. He was impressed by the way they sat their horses. Very straight. They rode with an ease that the Duke envied. He had never seen a European ride quite like that. "I've been told that the Plains Indians are the finest light cavalry in the world," he whispered back to Raider.

"Yeah. They can do more things with a horse than you'd believe."

The Duke was entranced by the Black Hills. He didn't even mind the lack of hunting. Raider had forbidden the firing of weapons until there was no longer any danger of running across potentially hostile Indians. The Duke even seemed to lose interest in the skins riding with the pack animals. He was slowly beginning to learn that the most important part of an expedition of this kind was not the animals killed or the trophies one took back home but the very trip itself, the closeness to the land, the quiet, the freedom, the sense of living with the earth.

There was a certain sense of disappointment, then, when they came in sight of Deadwood. They rode out onto a rise and there it was below them, the usual ugly little frontier settlement, a collection of wooden shacks, tents, lean-tos, dusty streets, and scruffy men. Deadwood was particularly unattractive because it was a boom town. Every get-rich-quick artist who'd had the guts to brave this particular corner of Indian country was down there scratching for money.

"Like I told you," Raider said to the Duke as they rode down toward the town, "when Custer was raidin' up this way a coupla years ago, they found gold. That's why there's a town down there."

"What's all that over in that direction?" the Duke asked, pointing to huge piles of earth and debris outside the town.

"That's the Homestake mine. Three real go-getters homesteaded five square miles o' land. Let's see, I think there was George Hearst, a man named Trevis, an' I can't remember the name of the other one. Hagger, or somethin' like that. The ore's pretty low grade, but there's a passel of it. The guess is that they'll be workin' the Homestake for the next hundred years."

They rode down into the town's center, which consisted mostly of mining supply stores, saloons, gambling halls, and houses of prostitution. Although it was only early afternoon, a steady stream of dusty, thirsty miners moved in and out of the various establishments.

"Wait'll you see the place at night," Raider said. "Real wild."

They headed for the livery stable, to have their animals taken care of. Then it was time to take care of themselves. Raider would just as soon have made camp out under the stars, but if they slept in the open it'd be too easy for somebody to sneak up on them at night. Raider had little doubt that von Bock and his men would show up eventually. If they'd backtracked and taken the long way around, that should be in a day or two. Yes, it would be a good idea to look for some nice private rooms for himself and the Duke.

Raider chose adjoining rooms on the top floor of a new but already dilapidated clapboard building. There was only one window in each room, and those windows were three stories up the side of a sheer wall. No easy way in through the windows. And it would be difficult to pussyfoot up the stairs; they creaked like hell.

After depositing their gear, then cleaning up, Doc and the Duke went out into the streets. Evening was coming on; the sky to the west was a gorgeous magenta color, with the few trees on the hills around the town sharply outlined against the last of the western light.

The bad news was that the local law was no friend of Raider's. "That damned kid, Wyatt Earp, has the job," Raider groused to the Duke.

"He's not a good man?"

"Well, not all that bad. I knew him when he was a town policeman in Wichita. The problem is, he's a bully. He's got a yen for beatin' people up, pistol-whippin' 'em. But what he really likes is gettin' his name in the newspaper. It was Bat Masterson who did most of the real law-work in Wichita. Now, there's a real man. If Bat was here, our worries'd be over."

They found Earp in one of the saloons, playing poker. He was a big man, in his late twenties, with flat cold eyes and a large drooping mustache. He was wearing a black suit with a string tie. A heavy Colt Peacemaker was thrust into his waistband. He'd just finished his hand, and the other players were drifting away. There was a big pile of chips in front of Earp. "Raider," he said coolly, looking up from his chair. "What brings you over this way?"

Raider sat down at the table. The Duke sat next to him. "Trouble," Raider said.

"I already figured that much," Earp replied in an emotionless voice. His cold flat eyes moved back and forth between Raider and the Duke.

"Yeah. Well . . ." Raider introduced the Duke and then went on to explain their problem with von Bock and company.

Earp listened without interrupting, toying with a pack of cards. When Raider had finished, he riffled the cards and began dealing himself a hand of seven-card stud. "Well," he finally said, "don't see as how there's much for the law to do—unless this von Bock character makes some overt move."

"You mean, like if they shoot the Duke," Raider said acidly.

"Uh-huh. Something like that."

Raider stood up. "Thanks for your time, Earp. See you around."

"Yeah. But Raider, no trouble while you're in town. You're a little too quick with your gun."

Raider remained for a moment looking down at the other man. "You just keep that in mind, Earp." Then he turned and walked away, the Duke right behind him.

"He certainly wasn't much help," the Duke said when they were once again outside. "Do you think that maybe he's afraid of von Bock?"

"Nope. One thing about Wyatt—he may be an asshole, but he ain't no coward. Maybe it's my fault. I don't like Earp, an' I've never made a secret out of it. He wouldn't do much cryin' if I got myself shot. Course, who knows? He might actually lend us a hand if it comes down to a shoot-out with von Bock. When Earp's the law in a place, he hates like hell to see anybody break the peace."

If he'd been on his own, Raider would simply have faced down von Bock. But his mission was to protect the

Duke, and the best way to do that was to stay away from fights. That was the real problem, keeping the Duke out of trouble, because the Duke, perhaps influenced by the wild frontier life around him, seemed increasingly ready for his own showdown with Von Bock.

They began to wander along the street. It was fully dark now, and the town was roaring. Loud tinny piano music poured out of the saloons and cathouses. The gambling dens were a little quieter, to allow concentration; men were hard at work over the braize tables. Raider and the Duke were walking by a card room when Raider suddenly saw a familiar figure. "Hey!" he said to the Duke. "Things are all of a sudden lookin' up."

Raider pushed his way in through the batwing doors. "Bill," he called out to a man standing by the bar.

The man turned. He was very tall, with a narrow, gaunt face and long blond hair that was beginning to turn gray. He was dressed in a fringed buckskin coat, pinstripe trousers, a silk shirt, and a string tie. An old-fashioned .36-caliber Navy Colt cap-and-ball pistol rode in a soft leather holster on his right hip. He spun around quickly when he heard Raider call his name, his long graceful fingers hovering near the butt of the Colt.

Then his face lit up. "Raider!" he said, smiling. "What hole have you been hiding in? Or did the gophers throw you back?"

There was a little more joshing, then Raider introduced the Duke to the tall stranger. "Duke, this here's Wild Bill Hickok. We been in some real scrapes together, me an' Bill, but I always managed to get him out in one piece."

"Bullshit, you lyin' bastard," Wild Bill replied good-naturedly. "Say, you ready to get skinned? Let's play us some cards."

The Duke managed to get himself included in the game, which was a disaster to his bankroll but otherwise a delight. Like many outsiders who'd read about the West, he'd heard a great deal about Wild Bill Hickok. And now here he was, Wilhelm, a simple German grand duke, playing cards with a genuine western gunfighter in a genuine saloon in a genuine mining town. It was well worth the two hundred dollars he dropped during the game, most of it going to Wild Bill, a little of it to Raider.

Made mellow by this unexpected windfall, Wild Bill listened to Raider's account of his troubles with von Bock. He made no promises, but by the time Raider and the Duke were back in their rooms—at four o'clock in the morning —Raider knew that they were no longer alone.

It was no surprise to Raider when von Bock showed up the next afternoon, looking weary, dirty, and very, very unhappy. Raider watched out of his hotel room window as the Count and his men walked their exhausted mounts down Deadwood's main street. They'd obviously been riding like hell.

Raider immediately went to the Duke's room to give him the bad news, and to suggest that he stay inside the hotel for the rest of the afternoon. The Duke refused, but by the time he hit the street, with Raider right behind him, von Bock and company had disappeared into one of the town's other hotels.

Raider steered the Duke toward the saloon where they'd met Hickok the night before. Sure enough, Wild Bill was already there, playing poker with several other men. He was facing away from the door, but Raider recognized him by his long hair and fringed buckskin jacket.

Raider walked up behind him. "Kinda surprises me to see an old warrior like you sittin' with your back to the door, Bill," Raider said to Hickok.

Hickok shrugged. "Oh, I'm through with that kinda thing, old friend. Gettin' too old. Besides, didn't I ever tell you that I got eyes in the back of my head. I knew all the time that you were back there tryin' to sneak up on me. Or maybe it's just my nose an' I smelled you comin'."

They both laughed over that, then got down to poker. Wild Bill was happy to have the Duke sit in on the game;

he liked easy money. They had been playing for about half
an hour when von Bock walked in through the door, followed by three other men—the gunfighters and Manteufel.

Raider pushed his chair back a little. "There's maybe
gonna be a little trouble, Bill. Those are the dudes I told
you about."

Hickok turned his head. Von Bock was standing near
the bar, but his men were fanning out to face the table
where Raider and the Duke were sitting. "Wittgenstein!"
Von Bock called out.

A look of annoyance flickered over Hickok's face.
"Keep it down," he said quietly. "We got a game goin'
here."

Von Bock dismissed Hickok with a contemptuous look.
"Wittgenstein," he called out again. "I'm speaking to you.
Are you deaf, man, or just afraid? But I see that you're
armed."

The Duke was wearing the .44 Raider had bought for
him. He slowly stood up, his face flushed with anger.
Manteufel and the two gunnies moved a little closer, their
faces eager, their hands near the butts of their guns.

Then Raider and Hickok stood up too. The other card-
players at the table suddenly discovered that they had other
things to do, and scattered. "You've interrupted our game,"
Hickok said quietly to von Bock. It was a cold, menacing
quietness, promising death.

Raider moved around to his left, so that he was on one
side of the Duke, Wild Bill on the other. There was more
movement behind them as the other occupants of the saloon began hunting for cover.

Von Bock had moved away from the bar to range himself with Manteufel and the two gunmen. Except that the
two gunmen were suddenly looking very nervous. "Hey,"
one of them said to Von Bock. "You didn't tell us Wild Bill
Hickok would be a part o' this."

A look of annoyance passed over von Bock's face. Then
the other gunman put in his two cent's worth. "Yeah! An' I

know that other one, too. He's a Pink. Even if we get the bastard, the Pinks are gonna be after our asses till hell freezes over."

"But you ain't *gonna* get me, are you, asshole?" Raider said in a silky voice. "Unless you want to try it. Come on, make your move. Make it now."

His right hand had drifted toward the butt of his .44. Wild Bill already had one hand resting on the smooth walnut grips of his .36. The duke's hand was dropping down toward his Remington.

"Uh-uh," the first gunman said. "I don't want no part o' this."

He abruptly turned and headed for the door. The second gunman hesitated a second longer, looking Raider straight in the eye, wondering if maybe he should try it after all. He'd been offered a lot of money. But what the hell good was money to a dead man? Yeah, this whole thing was looking too damn much like suicide. Shrugging, the second gunman spun on his heel and followed his companion outside.

That left only von Bock and Manteufel. They were now outnumbered, and they knew it. Von Bock's face was filled with an icy anger, but he had too much intelligence to throw his life away just for the sake of appearances. Turning toward the bar, he shouted for the bartender, then ordered a drink.

Manteufel, however, refused to turn away from the three men facing him. Raider grudgingly admitted to himself that the man was either very brave—or very stupid.

"Wittgenstein," Manteufel called out, although his eyes never left Raider. "How is that whore of yours—the one with the soft breasts?"

He said it in English, so that everyone in the bar would hear the insult. The Duke flushed and took a half step forward.

"No, he's mine," Raider insisted softly.

He walked toward Manteufel. He would have to take

the man on or chance the Duke taking him on, and he suspected that Manteufel would kill the Duke. "How ya doin', scarface?" he said coldly. "Last time I saw you, you were kissin' the floor—with my foot on the back o' your neck. Remember?"

"Oh, yes, I remember," Manteufel replied in a low, murderous voice. "And now you will pay for that insult. To strike a Prussian officer . . ."

"Well, I'm doin' it again," Raider said, suddenly stepping in close and backhanding Manteufel across the face.

Manteufel staggered back, rubbing his cheek. Raider's blow had left a livid red mark. Raider hoped that the man would come unglued, that he would go crazy and reach for his gun, and then Raider would kill him, thus wiping out one more of von Bock's dogs. He'd been aware of the Prussian's arrogant pride from the first time they'd met, in St. Louis, in Tony Faust's. Raider did not think Manteufel would be able to maintain his equilibrium after being struck in the face in front of a roomful of people.

But to Raider's surprise, Manteufel actually smiled. A smile of triumph. "You have struck me," he said. "You have challenged me to fight."

"Well, give the man a cigar," Raider said in an almost friendly voice. "You bet your ass I have."

"Good. I accept."

"That's fine with me. Now go for your gun."

Manteufel slowly shook his head, still smiling. "No. It is you who have challenged me. Therefore, I have the choice of weapons. Is that not so?" he asked von Bock and the Duke.

Both men nodded, the Duke very reluctantly. "We ain't in your bailiwick now," Raider snapped. "Go for your gun or get out."

"What's the matter?" Manteufel jeered. "Are you afraid? But then, there are no women for you to hide behind this time, are there?"

That last jibe was unfair, since it was Manteufel who

had pushed the fight when Sophie and Emma were present. Nevertheless Manteufel's words irritated Raider. He was also irritated by the murmur of agreement from the onlookers. "All right, you arrogant bastard," he snarled. "You go ahead and choose the weapons."

The Duke was shaking his head no, but Manteufel, smiling triumphantly, said quickly, "Sabers. In five minutes. Outside."

There was a cheer from the onlookers. Anything for a show. Raider had little choice but to nod his acceptance or back down in front of everyone. He knew that if he didn't fight Manteufel now, he'd lose all local support for protecting the Duke. Even Wild Bill was looking rather amused by the way things were turning out.

Raider nodded to Manteufel. "Okay. Let's get on with it."

They trooped outside, Raider, the Duke, Wild Bill, von Bock, Manteufel, and about twenty onlookers.

"Back there—behind the buildings," Manteufel said, pointing to a flat cleared space next to the livery stable.

Raider nodded, then began walking in that direction, Manteufel at his side. The crowd moved with them, attracting the curiosity of others. Soon there were over fifty people formed up in a big circle around the area where Raider and Manteufel stood, facing one another.

Meanwhile, von Bock had gone to fetch the sabers. While they were all waiting for him to return, the Duke moved next to Raider. "Let me stand in for you," he said in a low voice. "I suspect I have more experience with that kind of weapon."

"Uh-uh. I wanna kill the bastard myself."

The lugubrious look on the Duke's face mirrored his belief that it would be Manteufel doing the killing, but the Duke had the grace to keep the actual words to himself. Five minutes later von Bock arrived with two sheathed sabers. He held them out to Raider, hilt first. Raider chose one and drew it from its scabbard. The long blade hissed out into the open, glittering in the fading light of the sun, which was now quite low on the horizon. It would soon be dark.

Raider took a few practice swings with the saber while the crowd cheered. Being Americans, they tended to root for the underdog, and Raider was definitely the underdog. Manteufel had by now taken his weapon, and the expert manner in which he wielded the saber contrasted sharply with Raider's clumsier hacking.

Just as they were about to square off, Raider suddenly tossed the saber aside. "Too damn new a toy for me to start playin' with at a time like this," he said. Then he drew his bowie. "I know this old friend one hell of a lot better."

"No, Raider," the Duke burst out. "He'll have the reach on you."

"Maybe. Maybe not," Raider replied, carving the air in front of him with the huge knife.

The crowd cheered. They were now one-hundred-percent behind Raider. But that in itself wouldn't be enough to keep him alive. As both men faced one another and fell into the on-guard position, it was clear from the expression of malevolent anticipation on Manteufel's face that he intended to kill his opponent.

Manteufel lunged, attacking, feinting, thrusting. Raider tried to fight back, but Manteufel's blade suddenly flicked out toward his face. Raider jumped back, desperately parrying with the bowie knife. Steel rang against steel. Manteufel laughed, then lunged again, this time going for the body. Once again, Raider barely managed to parry the blow.

Then Manteufel grew overconfident. The next time he lunged, Raider not only parried but countered, leaping forward, his heavy blade beating aside Manteufel's longer but lighter blade, nearly knocking it from his hand. The bowie's broad point slashed to within an inch of Manteufel's face. "I'll put a scar on the other side," Raider panted, grinning.

Now Manteufel grew a little more cautious. Within another couple of minutes he had clearly shown the superiority of his fencing skills. Raider was continually pressed back, with Manteufel's saber building a flickering fence of steel in front of him, the tip darting in closer and closer.

During one lunge, Manteufel pricked Raider on the left shoulder. Everyone sensed that Manteufel could have lunged in deeper, that he could have hit Raider in the center of the body. He could have killed him. The Prussian was beginning to play with Raider, the way a cat plays with a mouse.

Raider was by now completely on the defensive. Only the desperation of his defense and the weight of his blade kept Manteufel from finishing him off. Finally, it looked like the end was near. Manteufel had surged forward, mounting a final blistering attack, his saber slashing, lunging, feinting. Raider staggered backwards, and then appeared to lose his balance. He stumbled badly, his arms flung out to the side for balance, his bowie no longer protecting his body.

With a snarl of triumph, Manteufel lunged forward, the point of his saber aimed straight at Raider's heart. But Raider, who had faked the loss of balance, quickly leaped to one side, and before Manteufel could correct his aim, Raider whipped his arm back and threw the bowie with all his strength.

Committed to his lunge, Manteufel was unable to move out of the way or to use his saber to beat the knife aside. With a meaty *thunk,* the heavy blade buried itself in his chest.

Manteufel staggered back, a look of disbelief on his face. He managed to hang on to his saber for another couple of seconds, then it slipped from suddenly nerveless fingers. Sinking slowly to his knees, Manteufel wrapped his hands around the bowie's hilt and tried to pull it out of his body. He finally looked up at Raider, his eyes huge, accusing. He held Raider's gaze for another second or two, then toppled forward onto his face, his fall driving the knife even further into his body.

"Foul! Foul!" Von Bock was shouting.

Raider turned toward him. "What the hell are you yellin' about?" he asked disgustedly.

"You cheated! You threw the knife! You broke the rules!" Von Bock screamed, his face crimson with anger.

Raider walked over to Manteufel and turned him over with his foot. The Prussian's eyes were open and staring. He was very dead. Raider bent down and tried to tug his knife loose. It had stuck fast in bone and would not come free until he placed one foot on Manteufel's chest and pulled hard.

Then, after wiping the blade on Manteufel's pants leg, Raider finally turned toward von Bock. "Rules?" he asked innocently. "In a knife fight? Well, nobody ever said anythin' to me about rules."

CHAPTER THIRTEEN

The crowd took Raider to the nearest saloon for a victory celebration. His star was riding high at the moment; he'd provided entertainment in a place otherwise devoid of entertainment.

Men shouted and cheered and slapped Raider on the back in between buying him drinks. Meanwhile, the Duke was standing by himself at the bar, a glass of beer in one hand. He couldn't stand the local whiskey. "Just like the old roman gladitorial games," he murmured bemusedly. "Blood on the sand . . . a cheering mob."

Von Bock was nowhere in sight, but Raider doubted that he had disappeared for good. Not a man like von Bock. He was obviously one of those humorless bastards that thought of nothing but duty first, last, and always. The kind of troublemaker that Raider loathed; they made life so hard for a man as lazy as himself. No, that damned German was not going to rest until the Duke was dead.

Pretty soon the party took on its own momentum, and nobody noticed when Raider and the Duke slipped away. Raider, somewhat the worse from all the cheap rotgut whiskey that had been poured down him, nevertheless took great care as he and the Duke negotiated back alleys toward their hotel.

They made it without incident. Raider immediately went to his room and flopped down on the bed. It had been one hell of a day. All during the fight he'd been pretty sure that Manteufel was going to kill him. He'd kept expecting that glittering length of cold steel to slide in between his ribs, or the razor sharp edge to split his skull. Not that he was complaining about the way it had turned out.

The question was, what next? For the time being they would probably be safe enough in Deadwood. Von Bock's local standing was now pretty low. He'd backed the wrong man in a fight. Besides, he was a foreigner who'd done very little to hide his contempt for the locals. The miners would back up Raider and the Duke.

Wyatt Earp had put in a belated appearance, somewhat irked by the killing, but since there had been no gunfire, and everyone assured him it had been a fair fight, he'd let the matter rest.

And then there was always Wild Bill. Quite a man to have on your side. But Raider and the Duke couldn't stay in Deadwood forever. Sooner or later they were going to have to hit the trail and head south toward Denver, to meet Doc. And once they were out in the open again, with nothing but wilderness around them . . .

The next morning began another day of poker, drinking, and slaps on the back from the locals, both for Raider and for the Duke. The Duke lapped it all up at first, but by the second day Raider could see that he was growing tired of Deadwood.

Well, so was Raider. He and the Duke sat down that afternoon and talked it over. The only conclusion they arrived at was a vague plan to slip out of town when von Bock wasn't watching. In the meantime they would try to give von Bock the impression that they were going to stay in Deadwood indefinitely.

For the next two days they saw nothing of von Bock. He seemed to have disappeared. Then Raider caught sight of him late the second night, sitting at a table in a saloon, bent over in very private conversation with a furtive-looking weedy little man. The bastard's probably looking for more help, Raider thought. But if that was the kind of man von

Bock was now recruiting, he must be pretty damned hard up.

However, the very next day he saw Von Bock on the street accompanied by several men of a very different stamp. There were the two gunfighters who'd backed down in front of Raider and Wild Bill, plus von Bock's two remaining Prussians, and three other men, real hardcase gunslinger types whom Raider had previously noticed hanging around the seedier saloons. From the way these newcomers wore their guns, Raider suspected they knew which end the bullet came out of. Real pros.

Obviously von Bock was getting ready to try something. But what? The situation hadn't changed that much. He doubted that von Bock's original two gunnies would ever work up the nerve to face both himself and Wild Bill. Maybe they were counting on numbers.

It was a clear warning that he and the Duke should continue sticking close to Wild Bill and the miners. Which was what the Duke was doing now. Raider had left him in the saloon with Hickok, donating more poker money. Raider headed in that direction.

He was still about fifty yards from the saloon when he caught sight of the weedy little man he'd seen von Bock talking to the night before. He was bent slightly forward, walking with a definite purpose, his right hand deep inside his coat pocket. And the bastard was heading straight toward the saloon where the Duke was playing cards with Wild Bill.

Raider broke into a run. The weedy little man was already going in through the swinging doors. Raider leaped toward the doors, reaching for his .44. He was just in time to see the man walk up behind Wild Bill—who had his back to the door again—take out a small-caliber pistol, and pump one round into the back of Wild Bill's head.

Raider dashed forward, but by now several other men had surrounded the gunman. The pistol was torn from his hand and he was knocked to the floor. But even while they were kicking him, the man was shouting over and over, "I did it! I did it! I'm the man who gunned down Wild Bill Hickok!"

Raider rushed up to Wild Bill. His head was slumped forward onto the tabletop in a spreading pool of blood. Raider turned his friend's head to the side and looked into his face. The eyes were wide-open and staring. Wild Bill was dead, dead, dead.

He glanced up at the Duke, who, still seated on the other side of the table, was staring back at him in disbelief. "Come on, let's get the hell out of here," Raider snapped.

The Duke nodded and got up to follow. As they headed toward the door, Raider saw that one of the other men who'd been playing at the table was turning over Wild Bill's cards. "Full house," he called out to the room at large. "Aces and eights."

Raider said nothing to the Duke about having seen Wild Bill's killer with von Bock. If he knew that, the Duke would only blame himself for being the indirect cause of Wild Bill's death.

The thing was, he and the Duke no longer had Wild Bill to back them up in a confrontation with von Bock and his men. The time was coming to get the hell out of town. But damn it all, the livery stable was closed for the day. They couldn't get to their mounts. For the time being the best place for himself and the Duke would be their rooms. Tomorrow he'd round up the two half-breeds, who were still in town, and make plans for riding out as quietly as possible.

However, by the next day, quiet was a rare commodity in Deadwood. Mid-morning, a rider came tearing into town on a lathered-up horse that dropped dead a few seconds after its rider pulled it to a sliding, wobbling stop. The man half fell out of the saddle, so spent that at first he could hardly speak.

Then, speak he did. "It's Custer," he gasped. "Wiped out. Little Big Horn."

Raider, who was on his way back from breakfast, thought he recognized the man as one of Custer's civilian scouts, but under all those layers of sweat, dust, and fear it was hard to be sure.

A considerable crowd was gathering around the man, and questions began to fly. He was made to repeat and repeat his story, because at first no one would believe what he was saying.

"I'm tryin' to tell you dumb apes!" the man shouted in exasperation, having got his wind back by now. "They're all dead! The whole fuckin' Seventh Cavalry—wiped out! God, there was so many Indians—*thousands* of the fuckers. They surrounded Custer when he rode down into the valley. I was over on the other side o' the hill, scoutin'. Custer'd heard there was some tepees in the valley, an' he went in to wipe 'em out, like he usually does, but when he got there . . . Jeez! I looked over the hill an' every Indian in the world musta been down there, war paint on, chargin' in hard an' whoopin' like fiends straight outta hell."

The man went on to tell how he'd laid low for over an hour, until the shooting had stopped. The next time he'd looked over the hill, the Indians were still down below—in the midst of hundreds of blue-clad bodies. "Nary a trooper made it outta there alive," the man murmured, his voice very clear in the stunned silence. "The Seventh Cav just ain't there no more."

"All of 'em?" a man asked incredulously.

"Yeah. Every man jack. I suppose so, anyhow. Custer'd split up his command, sendin' Major Reno off on his own. but I heard shootin' over that way, too. I guess they got Reno like they got Custer."

"Then there's nothin' between us an' them redskins but some real estate!" another man shouted, panic making his voice crack.

"You said there was thousands of Indians?" another man shouted, equally panicked.

It was chaos after that, every man on his own. All public order broke down as men scrambled to arm themselves, every one of them expecting a horde of warriors to come thundering over the hill at any moment.

Raider corraled the Duke. "This is our chance to get the hell outta here," he said. "Nobody'll notice us leavin' in all the excitement."

Raider rounded up the two half-breeds and sent them to the livery stable to saddle the stock. He wanted to go with them, but the Duke insisted on returning to the hotel first to settle their bill. Cursing all this noble honesty, Raider went with him. Of course, they couldn't find the desk clerk; he was out panicking himself like everybody else. Raider grabbed a wad of the Duke's money and tossed it onto the desk. Then, collaring the Duke, he led him out the front door—and almost into the arms of von Bock and his men.

They were coming down the street, all eight of them, von Bock, his two Prussians, and the five gunfighters he'd managed to accumulate. Raider and the Duke were out in the open on the boardwalk when von Bock spotted them. "There they are!" the big Prussian shouted, reaching for his pistol, which prompted his men to reach for theirs. Lead was about to fly.

CHAPTER FOURTEEN

Raider made no attempt to go for his gun. Instead, as the first bullets from von Bock's gang began chipping splinters from the hotel's wooden sides, he grabbed the Duke by the sleeve and hauled him into a narrow alley. "You hit?" he asked anxiously.

"No," the Duke replied, pulling out his .44 and turning back to face the entrance to the alley.

"Not here, goddamn it!" Raider said. "We'd be sittin' ducks!"

He propelled the Duke farther down the alley, to where a projecting outbuilding gave them some cover. "Okay, let 'er rip," he said to the Duke, crouching behind the outbuilding and leveling his Remington.

Three of von Bock's men had run into the alley's entrance. "That's stupid," Raider muttered, opening fire, sending lead down the alley as fast as he could cock and fire.

The Duke, crouched next to him, did the same. One of the attackers flew straight backward, propelled by the force of the heavy slugs that had ripped into his chest and neck. Another yelped and clasped a hand to his left arm, which was spurting blood. The third had the sense to turn around and sprint for the main street.

Grinning, the Duke was beginning to reload his revolver.

"Do it while we're movin'," Raider snapped, pulling him to his feet.

"But we have such good cover here."

"Sure. Until they get around behind us."

They walked quickly down a side alley, shucking empties out of their pistols and sliding in fresh rounds.
"Damn," Raider muttered, looking behind him. A trail of
brass marked the direction they had taken. "Come on, let's
go this way."

"But that's away from the livery stable."

"Yeah, but I bet they're closing off that route already."

Sure enough, Raider could hear the pounding of boots
from each end of the alley they had just left. A figure
suddenly showed in the alleyway behind them. Raider
snapped off a quick shot. This time their opponent was
more careful; he ducked behind cover and returned the fire,
forcing Raider and the Duke to break into a run. As they
dodged around a corner they could hear the man shouting
for reinforcements.

"This ain't no good," Raider panted. "If we keep on
runnin' this way, they'll just hunt us down. We gotta take
this war to them."

"You mean . . . gain the initiative."

"Yeah. Hey! You talk kinda like Doc."

Trying to remember the layout of the town, Raider
worked his way back toward the main street, but not so
quickly that they totally broke contact with their pursuers.
He had a plan.

The plan depended on the bulk of von Bock's force following them as a group. Which was why he and the Duke
would run along a little ways, then turn back to snap off a
couple of shots. This caused von Bock's men to bunch up
and come on cautiously.

Finally they were back at Deadwood's main street,
having ducked their way through the shanties, shacks, and
false-front frame buildings that made up the town. And it
looked like Raider's plan was working. Von Bock's men
had been funneled into an area full of scattered junk and
small storage sheds. Raider and the Duke now took up

positions covering this rather broken area, hunkered down out of sight.

Von Bock's men cautiously took up their own positions, hiding behind all the junk and debris so that they could cover the main street. They had learned to respect their opponents' marksmanship. And as the first man showed his nose, Raider opened up with two well-aimed shots that drove him back under cover.

There was a mad scramble for positions, with von Bock's men burrowing deep, snapping off their own shots in return. Raider and the Duke kept peppering away at them, making them keep their heads down. So far down that almost nothing of them showed, just the puffs of white smoke from their guns.

Of course, all this firing had not gone unnoticed. Heads were poking out of doorways and windows, and a lot of guns were showing. The townspeople were, after all, still in a panic over the Indian situation.

Which panic Raider now capitalized on. "Injuns!" he bellowed, pointing toward the area where von Bock and company were hiding. "Snuck into town. I saw 'em scalp three women back in them alleys!"

Men came pouring out into the street, all of them armed to the teeth. Taking cover, they began blasting away at the supposed "Indians" that Raider and the Duke had been shooting at.

There were howls of fear from von Bock's men as the storm of lead swept over their hiding place. Howls which, to the frightened townsmen, sounded like wild savages yipping for their blood. The firing went on and on, not doing too much damage, because von Bock's men had good cover, but there was no way they were going to be able to move out of there until they'd convinced the jumpy townspeople that they were not Indians.

Raider quickly led the Duke toward the livery stable. Their mounts were ready and waiting for them, saddlebags in place, packhorses loaded. The two half-breeds, however, citing the difficulties they had already had in Raider's employ, refused to accompany him and the Duke, for which Raider could not blame them. He paid them off and sent them on their way. Then he and the Duke swung up onto their mounts and headed out of Deadwood.

By the time they had climbed the hill at the edge of town, the firing behind them had slackened off. Then it stopped altogether. "They'll be on our trail soon," Raider said.

"If there's any of them still alive."

"Oh, there will be. Most of them townies couldn't hit the side of a barn if they was inside it. They'll be comin' after us, but it'll take 'em some time to find our trail. So let's make tracks."

Raider had considered taking the long way around, north and west, heading north of the Black Hills into Wyoming, and then straight south toward Colorado. But he now decided that they would be harder to track in the rougher terrain of the hills, so he angled off in a direction that was more south than west.

They pushed the animals hard, making many miles before nightfall caught them. They rode more slowly after dark, picking their way carefully, since Raider didn't want to end up trapped in some dead-end canyon. It was after midnight when they finally made camp.

Raider awoke the next morning to find the Duke already up and starting a fire to make coffee. "Uh-uh," Raider said, jumping up out of his bedroll and throwing dirt on the flames.

"Why did you do that?" the Duke snapped, obviously angry.

"You're forgettin' about the Injuns," Raider replied. "It's gonna be all-out war after what they did to Custer. The Injuns ain't dumb; they know that, an' if they find us, they're gonna shoot first and talk about it later. So no fires, no noise, an' no showin' ourselves."

After a cold breakfast, they loaded the animals and continued on. "Why don't we leave the pack animals?" the Duke said. "They slow us down."

"We may need 'em later."

"But how?"

"I don't know yet."

They were traveling very cautiously now. They had entered the part of the Black Hills most sacred to the Indians. Raider made certain that they never outlined themselves against a skyline. Sometimes, when they came to the edge of an open area, he would insist they stop for an hour or more, while he sat his horse, unmoving, trying to *feel* if there was anyone observing that open space.

Despite all their precautions they were finally ambushed by a small party of Sioux just a few miles short of leaving the hills. There were six of them, and they were in position before Raider realized they were there. He and the Duke had been caught in the middle of a small cleared space, with high ground all around. They'd been forced onto that part of the trail because of the pack animals.

Raider's first instinct, when he realized the Indians were there, was to whip up the horses and run them fast toward cover. But he doubted they'd make it. The Indians had too good a drop on them, and even if they did make it to cover, they'd be trapped, with more and more Indians eventually showing up, until they were finally overrun and dug out.

"Stop your horse. Don't move a muscle," Raider hissed to the Duke.

"Why . . . what . . . ?"

"Shut up!"

Raider then held up his right hand, palm out, and called out in Lakota Sioux—God, he hoped they were Sioux— "Show yourselves, my brothers. We are not here to fight."

Silence. Utter silence. Which was better than the sudden blasting of guns and the whistle of bullets. But still, it was the kind of silence that could half kill a man with tension.

"We bring gifts," he called out again.

Which did the trick. Indians were big on gifts. There was a slight rustling in the bush above them, and the six warriors rode out into the open, three on one side, three on the other. Their rifles were pointed unwaveringly at Raider and the Duke.

Raider slowly dismounted, motioning for the Duke to do the same. To the Indians it would look as if the two white men were at a considerable disadvantage, being on foot, but Raider knew that if it came to a shoot-out in this narrow space, being on the ground might tip the odds a little more in their favor. If any shooting started, they could hide behind their horses, and the Indians' horses would probably spook a little from all the noise, spoiling their riders' aim.

But Raider didn't want the situation to deteriorate to the point where there was shooting. He quickly singled out the warrior that looked like he had the most clout and addressed him in Lakota. "We have no wish to fight our Sioux brothers."

The warrior rode closer, until he was sitting his horse only ten yards away. "If you do not want to fight the Sioux, what are you doing in our mountains?"

"We have gifts."

"Gifts?" the warrior said with a sneer. "We can take what you have anytime we want."

"That may not be as easy as you think," Raider snapped back. The worst thing he could do would be to show weakness or fear. He had to balance off respect against the desire to fight, which was the Indians' favorite sport. He also had to balance off the Indians' natural propensity to steal against their desire to receive gifts. Stealing was fun; getting gifts was flattering. Killing was fun; recognizing bravery was noble. Raider knew he was working with a very basic and rather childish ethic. The thing was to work it well.

"What gifts do you have?" the warrior abruptly asked.

"Skins, knives, guns, powder, and shot."

The warrior sneered down at Raider. "And why do you come here with gifts, white man? Is it because you fear the fighting men of the Lakota Nation?"

Raider matched the warrior's cold stare. "I fear no man," he replied acidly. "Push me far enough and you'll find that out . . . you and me . . . man to man. I come with gifts because I honor the Sioux. A people with whom I once lived."

The other warriors had now ridden closer. One of them, an older man, suddenly spoke. "Hah!" he burst out. "I recognize you now. You are the one we called 'Man Whose Gun Never Misses'!"

Raider nodded, watching for the reaction of the first warrior he'd spoken to. This was the man whose actions would determine the actions of the others. Raider saw a combination of respect and curiosity in his eyes. The respect was there because of Raider's Indian name, which indicated that he was good with a gun, which could materially effect this Indian's health if it came down to a fight. And then there was curiosity about a white man who had lived with the Sioux.

The older Indian was speaking excitedly to the others. "This man lived with my band for over two years. He was a great hunter and fighter. He was also a good friend of our people. He gave us much good advice about the white man. He saved the lives of many Lakota."

The first warrior continued looking down at Raider, his eyes now completely inscrutable. "Show us the gifts," he finally said.

Raider went to the pack animals and began unloading the packs. First he laid flat some of the skins of the animals the Duke had killed, then covered them with odds and ends from the packs, including the two Sharps rifles, the skinning knives, and several boxes of ammunition. All this bounty was too much for the warriors; they were soon off their horses and crowding around, talking excitedly as they fingered the goods.

Raider picked up the two rifles and handed one to the hard-nosed warrior, whose name, he now learned, was Dull Ax. The other Sharps went to the older warrior, Broken Thumb.

Dull Ax worked the action of the Sharps several times before tossing it aside contemptuously. "It shoots only one time. I will keep my gun of many bullets."

Dull Ax was carrying a Winchester lever-action '66 repeater. Raider was glad he'd turned down the Sharps. While the Winchester fired more shots, you could pot a man with the Sharps at a much greater distance. He didn't like the idea of seeing a rifle like that in the hands of a warrior as bellicose as Dull Ax.

However, some of the other gifts softened up Dull Ax. He took two skins and the best of the skinning knives. There was also a pint bottle of whiskey. In a few minutes it was making the rounds of the warriors.

"Thank God it ain't a quart," Raider muttered to the Duke.

"Why?"

"'Cause a quart'd drive 'em wild, killin' crazy. This little bit'll just loosen 'em up."

Doc had explained to him once that the red man had not had the thousands of years of exposure to alcohol that the white man had. They had no built-up tolerance. "Thousands of years ago it drove white people crazy too," Doc had told him. "It was used as a sacramental drug during religious ceremonies. People went completely out of their heads and had visions."

Which was what normally happened to Indians when they drank. And their visions usually included killing. However, the pint of whiskey, which had not even been full, soon had them in a state of hilarious friendliness.

"Thank you for the gifts," Broken Thumb said, weaving slightly. "Now maybe we can do something for you. For instance, did you know about the six white men and the Indian following your trail?"

"Well, it don't surprise me much."

"They are your enemies?"

"They are enemies of all good men."

"Hah! We will fight them, then. For one thing, that Indian with them is an Arapaho, and the Arapaho are our enemies."

Dull Ax had held himself somewhat apart, maintaining a rather ponderous dignity. But now, at the prospect of a fight, his face lit up. He'd been cheated out of scalping these two strange white men, but now another opportunity was presenting itself. "Yah-hah!" he screamed, vaulting onto the back of his horse. He was just drunk enough so that he nearly fell over the other side, much to his embarrassment, but he righted himself, swaying somewhat, and motioned to the others to follow him. "Death to the white eyes!" he shouted.

The other warriors quickly mounted. Broken Thumb, the most sober, took up the reins of the packhorses; Raider had insisted that they take them, which they would have done anyhow. "At the very least we will make those men go back the way they came," Broken Thumb said. He smiled then. "Goodbye, Man Whose Gun Never Misses. It is good to remember the old days."

"Yes, it is."

And then the Indians galloped off, taking most of Raider and the Duke's possessions with them. But not their lives, thank God.

"Okay, let's get the hell out of here before they change their minds," Raider said to the Duke as he swung up into the saddle.

They were about a quarter of a mile away when they heard the sound of heavy firing behind them, accompanied by the shrill whooping of the Indians. "Well, that's the end of von Bock," the Duke said. "I'm rather sorry that he had to end his life that way."

"Don't count him out yet. If those bucks can wipe him out in the first rush, then they will. But if von Bock an' his men dig in, there'll be a lot of shootin' until the Injuns get bored with it all, an' then they'll just ride off an' look for somethin' else to do. One thing, though—I got a feelin' von Bock will have had enough of the Black Hills. We'll make it outta here easy now—if we don't meet up with any more Sioux."

As they rode along, Raider lapsed into a deep silence. The meeting with the warriors had brought back memories of his life with the Lakota Sioux. For two years he'd lived with Broken Thumb's small band. Two years of living freer than he'd ever imagined a man could live. Two years of hunting and wandering, accompanied by what was really a large family. But it was also two years of constant daily warfare.

The young men of the village regularly rode out in small bands, partly to search out hunting grounds, partly to see if they could find other Indians to steal from. Or to fight and kill. Every moment was alive with danger. No camp could be made without the possibility of some other tribe, even another subgroup of the Lakota, sneaking up on them and trying to take their hair. Every Indian outside of the immediate group was every other Indian's enemy. Except during the great annual tribal gatherings. It was a macho world of warriors, exciting to Raider at first, but later, when he'd matured a bit, rather repetitious.

He'd finally left the Lakota to take up the white man's life again, but he'd never been quite the same man. Memories of those gloriously free days, with nothing for a man to do but find food, boast, fight, and make love to Indian maidens, who knew how to please a warrior, would come back to him when he least expected it. It usually happened when he was in a town, or when he was unlucky enough to have a regular job.

Working for the Pinkerton Agency had helped; at least he was semi-free, and there was enough danger to keep his blood moving. However, there would never be any going back to the Lakota. Deep down he was too much of a white man. Besides, the old life barely existed any longer anyhow. It had been crushed by the Army, by men like Custer. Soon, perhaps in another ten years, there would be no free Indians left at all. Raider knew that he would not be able to accept the sorrow of watching that happen from too close up. Better to stay out of the way. That meant he'd have to live with white society for the rest of his life, or at least as close to it as he could stomach.

Just stay free, old son, he reminded himself as they began to ride out of the wonderful, magic Black Hills. "Hey!" he suddenly said, breaking the long silence that had developed between himself and the Duke. "I wonder what's happenin' with Doc an' the women? Livin' it up soft and easy, if I know Doc."

CHAPTER FIFTEEN

Life had indeed been quite pleasant aboard the train since Raider and the Duke had left it to head north. Before, the Duke had been the center of every action, every decision, from the direction the train traveled to the time for dinner. Everything had revolved around him. It was his train, his hunting trip, his women.

Now it was Doc, Sophie, and Emma who determined life's daily pace. It was only a hundred miles from Cheyenne to Denver, but no one was in a hurry. On a whim, Emma and Sophie decided that they wanted to take the majority of their daylight meals out-of-doors, so whenever the opportunity presented itself, the train was halted on some convenient siding and Doc and the women wandered off for a picnic, the servants humping the picnic supplies after them, then conveniently disappearing back into the train once the alfresco table service had been laid out on the grass and covered with whatever treats the chef had prepared.

Doc and the ladies sat or reclined on soft cushions, roughing it in the great outdoors European style, making do with smoked salmon, caviar, and the last of the buffalo tongue, washing this simple fare down with good clarets and hock, then lying back, replete, leisurely sipping the finest cognac and armagnac. Not an altogether unpleasant life.

An additional pleasure for Doc was his nearly uninterrupted closeness to Emma. They spent hours, nearly entire days together, and it was slowly becoming clear to Doc that Emma enjoyed this closeness nearly as much as he did.

It was clear to Sophie, too. She was already feeling the absence of a man in her bed, and for a while she toyed with the idea of taking Doc for herself, of seducing him the way she had seduced Raider. She decided against it, however, realizing that doing such a thing right under the nose of her lover's sister might not be the cleverest move, especially when it involved a man whom Emma herself was so obviously interested in.

The poor stupid little idiot, Sophie thought. Why doesn't she just take him? He's so ready! *Gott in Himmel!* It was maddeningly exasperating to see a fine-looking man like Doc go to waste, sexually speaking, simply because of Emma's well-bred hesitation about taking a step Sophie considered simple and natural.

Still, nothing compromising occurred. Doc was too polite, Emma too cautious. They continued on toward Denver in short hops, sometimes staying for an entire day in one place, picnicking. Nothing at all might have happened between them—had it not been for the kidnapping.

The last day out from Denver, their route took them near a lake; the land was dotted with lakes in this part of Colorado. Sophie and Emma insisted on having their daily picnic at the lakeshore, although it was more than a mile from the track. The engineer, of course, contributed his usual exhibition of grumbling and dire threats, although rather halfheartedly, now that he did not have the symbol of the Duke's dukeness to arouse his republican ire.

Therefore, the train was run onto a nearby siding, and orders were given to the chef to prepare the day's cold collation. Some rather nice wines were chosen, along with clothing suitable for the outing. And, merely an hour and a half later, the little caravan set off for the lakeshore, Doc and the two women walking out in front as if for a stroll in the park, while a line of servants followed behind, loaded down with enough supplies for a two-week safari.

Once the lakeshore was reached, the appropriate cloths were spread on the turf, cushions put down for the principals, and the food laid out as attractively as possible. The servants were then waved on their way back to the train. The lakeshore now belonged exclusively to Doc and the ladies.

It was a very lovely lakeshore, fringed with reeds, in which a multitude of birds had taken up residence, much to the delight of the women. The day was very lovely, a bit warm, actually, but not intolerably so, thanks to a light and pleasant breeze. The food was eaten with a particularly German gusto. Quite a bit of wine was consumed, and finally brandy was poured into cut-crystal snifters, ready for postprandial bliss. Ah, paradise indeed. There was now nothing to do but lie back and enjoy life.

Evening was slowly coming on, with the temperature now falling a bit. The fading light was glorious, turning the waving tufts of reed and grass a lovely golden tan. And the women were lovely. Doc sighed, torn between happiness and regret. The happiness had an obvious root; he was living in the most delightful luxury, his days spent close to Emma. Yes, paradise indeed. But the roots of the regret lay in the same place—the knowledge that, for him, it would all soon enough come to an end. This was a life he had merely been permitted to borrow for a short time. One he would have to make certain that he enjoyed to the fullest while it was still there to be enjoyed.

"I'm getting cold," Sophie said.

Doc, who had been exchanging unusually warm glances with Emma, pulled himself away from this pleasant task to take stock of the situation. It was indeed growing slightly chilly. And in another half hour it would be getting on toward dark. "I suspect it's time to start back," he said regretfully.

"Oh no," Emma burst out. "It's all too lovely. Let's stay here a while longer and watch the light go."

There was a new kind of glow on her face, and Doc

suspected that it had been initiated as much by his company as by the setting sun. That particular glow had been growing noticeably over the past couple of days. She wants me, Doc realized.

Therefore, unwilling to lose this momentary intimacy, and eager to let the evening work its magic, Doc committed a serious error of judgment. Under Sophie's prodding —she wasn't quite ready to leave yet either—he agreed to walk back to the train and fetch her shawl. He would also instruct the servants to follow half an hour later to fetch the picnic things.

Therefore, besotted by passion and the loveliness of the evening, Doc walked off toward the train, leaving the two women alone. This did not bother him the way it should have, since he did not consider for a moment that anything could really happen to them. They were, after all, in what seemed to be a completely uninhabited part of the country, free of people; and as everyone knows, it is man who is the most dangerous and murderous of all the animals.

He walked quickly back to the train, which took him less than twenty minutes. It took another ten minutes to send one of the maids for Sophie's shawl, and to instruct the servants. So he was on his way back toward the lake within half an hour after he'd left. He walked faster this time. By now he was a little concerned at how quickly it was growing dark.

He experienced a bad moment as he approached the lake, because he could not see the women. Then he reflected that the spot they had chosen for the picnic was in a little depression by the lakeshore that was not visible from more than a few yards away. An extremely private place. He began to curse the luck that would not permit him to be there alone with Emma.

Doc expected to see the women's heads pop up over the edge of the little depression at any moment. But they did not. He walked a little to one side, suspecting that he was off course, but a moment later he discovered that he had indeed been walking in the right direction. It was simply that the women were not there.

His first glance at the picnic sight suggested to him that Emma and Sophie were probably walking along the lake-shore. Accordingly, he called their names, but got no answer. Then he took a closer look at the ground around the remains of the meal they had shared and felt his heart lurch terribly.

The picnic sight had been churned up by several pairs of boots and mocassins. There were muddy boot prints on the picnic cloths. What had been left of the meal had obviously been pawed over. An empty cognac bottle lay on its side. It had been nearly full when he'd left.

And one of Sophie's shoes lay on the grass, its heel broken off.

A confused trail of footprints led off around one side of the lake. Doc ran along that trail, trying to read the signs the way Raider would have read them. It soon became clear that someone was being dragged along. Maybe two people. Emma and Sophie, of course. Someone had taken them!

Doc's first impulse was to run along the path and over-take the kidnappers. Fortunately, common sense stopped him. There were obviously several kidnappers, and he was carrying only his little .32. The wrong move now would probably only mean his death, without affecting any help at all for the women. He must control himself. He must not go off half-cocked.

Instead, he began to run back toward the train, thinking furiously as he ran. He'd need help, of course, but there was clearly no point in enlisting the servants. They were Europeans and had a servant's mentality. They would be useless. But on the other hand, the members of the train crew were old hands at the sudden episodes of violence that cropped up from time to time in the life of a railroader.

Doc was back at the train in ten minutes. Seeking out the engineer, he briefly filled him in. The engineer immediately called his crew together, another three men. As soon as they'd heard what had happened, the crew unanimously decided that all of them would go after Emma and Sophie.

So the five of them—Doc, the engineer, and the three crewmen—ran together into Raider and Doc's car and armed themselves. Doc picked up a double-barreled, ten-gauge shotgun, then began shoving shells into his coat pockets. The heavy Smith and Wesson .44 Russian that Raider had taken away from Manteufel during the confrontation in Tony Faust's Oyster House was lying at the bottom of the ammunition trunk. Doc quickly shoved the big pistol into his belt.

Within ten minutes of the time Doc had arrived back at the train, the little posse was on its way toward the lake, moving at a steady half trot. By the time they got to the picnic site, it was beginning to grow quite dark. One of the firemen, a grizzled veteran of various brushes with unhappy, homicidal Indians, took a critical look at the tracks that led around the side of the lake. "Whoever the bastards are, they're gonna be hard as hell to follow in this kinda light."

Doc could only agree, and his stomach twisted in dismay. Time was, of course, of the essence. The future of the women would be grim, once their kidnappers had an opportunity to stop their flight for long enough to . . . No, better not think about that.

What would Raider do in a situation like this? God, if he were only here now! But that kind of thinking wouldn't get them anywhere. It was all up to him and these four other men. He'd have to put his mind completely on the current problem. Agreed, it looked as if trying to follow the kidnappers' tracks would not work out very well. As it was, the land away from the soft moist earth around the lakeshore was damned hard, and probably wouldn't show much in the way of footprints anyhow.

If he could only figure out in which direction the kidnappers would head. His eyes raked the landscape, trying to see through the deepening gloom. "Over there," he suddenly said to the old fireman. "That opening in the hills."

There were foothills a couple of miles away. He'd glanced over in that direction earlier, when he'd been lazing on the ground next to Emma and Sophie, and he'd noticed sheer cliffs rising up toward the higher ground, broken at one point by a broad canyon leading up into the foothills. He couldn't make out much detail now, but the break in the cliffs was faintly visible.

The fireman nodded. "Yep. 'Bout the only place you could hide out around here."

So they headed for the canyon opening. It was a risk; the kidnappers might not have gone in that direction at all. From the tracks, they had appeared to be on foot, but they may have had horses tethered not far away. However, there was no point in thinking of possible disasters. This was probably the only hope they had of finding and saving the women.

The five of them moved quickly through the gathering dusk. It was full dark by the time they reached the opening into the canyon. Once inside, they at first saw nothing but an even deeper blackness—until they had penetrated far enough to see the fire.

It was in a little side canyon, about half a mile farther along, and invisible from the plain, which was probably what gave the kidnappers the bravado to light it in the first place. Homing in on that flickering light, Doc and the others were within a hundred yards of the fire in another few minutes. Then Doc held up a hand to signal a stop. "We'll have to be quiet from here on in," he whispered. "We don't know how many of them there are. We'll have to count on surprise. Keep on the lookout for a guard."

But there was no guard. All of the eight kidnappers were too interested in the women they had captured to take a turn at guard duty. They had seldom had a chance at women like these two, and not one of them was going to risk losing his share.

As Doc led the four railroad men closer to the fire, he had to resist an impulse to rush straight in and start killing. The scene around the fire enraged him. The kidnappers were standing in a circle around their two captives, swilling the leftover alcohol they'd taken from the picnic site and jeering at the women.

Both Sophie and Emma had obviously been ill treated; the top of Sophie's dress had been ripped half off her body, baring most of her breasts. Emma was bleeding slightly from a scratch on one cheek. They were standing very close together, obviously tense and frightened, but also appearing ready to fight. It looked as if they had already been trying to defend themselves.

As yet, the men were only toying with them. They could have overpowered the women anytime they chose, but that would have spoiled the game.

From time to time one of the grinning men would step in and make a grab at Sophie's breasts or try to drag Emma toward him. As Doc watched, one took hold of Emma's arm, ripping at the bodice of her dress. Emma strained away from her tormentor for a moment, then suddenly moved back toward him, throwing him off-balance while she clawed at his face. The man howled and leaped back, while his mates laughed. Blood was streaming from parallel lines of scratches on his right cheek.

The man snarled in rage, and would have rushed at Emma again had not one of the others grabbed him by the sleeve and pulled him back. "You had your chance, damn you," the other man snarled. "Now I want mine."

The kidnappers were a raggedy bunch of Army deserters, renegade half-breeds, and small-time bandits who normally holed up in the mountains, which explained their lack of horses. Horses did not do well on the precipitous slopes where the men had long ago been forced to flee.

Only occasionally did they make forays into the plains, and very seldom did they realize the kind of score they'd pulled off tonight.

The man who jerked the other one away from Emma was now moving toward her himself. "Come on, you stuck-up bitch," he taunted, grinning. "I'm gonna show ya what ya been missin' all your fuckin', rich-girl life."

Emma shrank back. The man followed, dragging it out. He feinted to one side, causing Emma to move away in the other direction. She was off-balance now, and the man stepped in quickly, reaching out to seize her by one arm, his other hand hooking into the top of her dress, ready to rip it down to her waist.

He was still grinning in anticipation when Doc walked in out of the darkness and cut him in half with a blast from one barrel of the big shotgun. While the man was still falling backward, a look of pure incredulity on his face, Doc blew the head off the only other kidnapper who'd so far had the presence of mind to reach for his gun.

Then the railroaders ran in, firing as fast as they could work the levers of their Winchesters. There was no safe way they could stay back in the dark and pick off the kidnappers from concealment. Not with the women right in amongst them.

Doc knew that he had no time to reload the shotgun, so he jerked the big Smith and Wesson .44 from his belt and began firing. There was a certain amount of firing coming back from the kidnappers now, but it lasted only a few seconds, until the last of them had been cut down by the concentrated firepower of their attackers. It had all happened too quickly for them to make an adequate defense against these yelling, shooting men who'd appeared so suddenly in their midst, while the kidnappers' minds were still on what they wanted to do to the women. Now they were dying, their bodies riddled with bullets.

It was suddenly silent, except for a last few shots to put to rest any of the bandits who were still moving. Emma and Sophie, stunned by this sudden reversal of their apparently hopeless situation, threw themselves into the arms of their rescuers. In fact, Sophie threw herself into the arms of several. But Emma headed straight toward Doc, who was now thrusting the .44 back into his belt. "Oh my God!" was all she could think to say, and then Doc's arms were around her and she was pressing herself tightly against him.

Doc liked that. He liked the feel of her softness, the warmth of her body. The agitation of her, the intense desperation of the way she was holding on to him, added an almost intolerable excitement. He pulled her closer. She responded with that same wild desperation.

And then it was time to go, time to head back toward the train; there was always the chance that there might be other men in the area like the men they'd just fought and killed.

Nothing was done to help any of the kidnappers who might still be alive. Such human garbage was not considered worth the effort. As for the attackers, only one man had been hit, and only superficially—a shallow wound in the upper arm.

The trip back to the train took much longer than the trip out; this time there was no urgency driving the men on. As soon as they were aboard, Doc gave the order to get underway. Then he took Emma straight to her sleeping room, while Sophie, barely bothering to hold the tattered upper portion of her dress in place, launched into a vivid description of her adventure for the benefit of the servants and those of the train crew whose presence was not absolutely necessary for the running of the train.

Even in the privacy of her room Emma continued to cling fiercely to Doc. "I thought I was going to die," she whispered. "I knew that it had to be death, because I would have had to make them kill me before I ever let them . . ."

Doc soothed the girl, easing her down onto her bed. He had no overt intention of doing anything other than comforting her, although his blood was scalding his veins as he felt her so close against him.

Oddly, it was Emma who eventually took the initiative. As so often happens in life-and-death situations, a sexuality had been born of the trauma. Emma clung ever more tightly to Doc, burying her face against his neck, pulling him down onto her, while her hands dug desperately into his back.

It didn't take Doc very long to realize the nature of Emma's reaction. He tried to hold himself back, to be a gentleman, but when it became unmistakably clear that she did not want him to hold back, he gave in, feverishly returning her caresses.

Later he could not remember either of them undressing, but suddenly they were both naked, her flesh hot against his. It was all instinct after that, a wild, desperate coupling that soon had Emma moaning and twisting under him, her eager cries filling his ears. Finally, the storm past, they collapsed together, skin to skin, slick with sweat, breathing heavily.

The next time was slower, more tender. They eagerly investigated one another's bodies, filled with the fascination of newness. They were able to laugh now, to play. This second time was the best.

When at last Emma lay sleeping against him, Doc remained awake, thinking, but sensing that for the time being he must not think too much. He must not dwell on the sure knowledge that this joining together could be for a little while only. Eventually, Emma the girl, Emma the lover, would become once again Emma, Countess of Vorburg.

CHAPTER SIXTEEN

Raider and the Duke sold their horses and gear in Cheyenne, then took the first available train to Denver. Much to Raider's surprise, the Duke insisted that he preferred riding second class. That was fine with Raider, so he and the Duke made their way to a seat in a car overflowing with cowboys, gamblers, farmers, drummers, entire families, and a dog or two.

All the way to Denver the Duke sat quietly on the hard wooden bench, observing his fellow passengers as if he had just discovered a new species. Raider was studying the Duke with an equal amount of interest. He'd been acting damned strange ever since Deadwood, like a man undergoing some kind of fundamental internal change. He seemed quieter, more reflective, more thoughtful. And at the same time, stronger.

It was quite a shock to the Duke when they arrived in Denver. Raider took it more in stride. He was accustomed to making the abrupt change from wide open spaces to smelly, clamorous cities. He genuinely despised the filthy, crowded, muddy streets, but accepted them grudgingly. After all, he would not have to stay in the damned place forever.

The Duke, however, reacted with confused disgust. He seemed particularly annoyed by the press of people. He finally pulled Raider into a saloon. "I can't face the women yet," he said as he ordered a whiskey. "I have to think."

Once again, the Duke's mood suited Raider just fine. And why not? Raider was thirsty and the Duke was buying. After half an hour, the Duke got up and headed toward the door. "All right. I'm ready."

It was not all that easy to find Doc and the women. Having been out of touch with them for so long, they had no idea where they were staying. Naturally, they looked for the train first, but when they found it, there was no one with it except for two hired guards. At first the guards tried to run off the two dusty, ragged trail bums who were prowling around this fancy train. Raider finally seized one of them by the throat and by dint of loud, threatening conversation convinced both guards that the Duke was indeed the train's owner.

But the guards did not know where Doc or the women might be. "They said they was goin' to a hotel" was all the men could tell them. Nor were they able to question the train crew; they were all in town, enjoying their unexpected holiday by doing their best to drink themselves to death.

The Pinkerton National Detective Agency's main western regional office was in Denver. For a while Raider was tempted to go to the office and see what they knew about Doc's whereabouts. But he really didn't want to do that. There would be questions on how the trip was going and what he and Doc were doing to protect the Duke. The idea of going to the office had occurred to him before; he'd told the Duke that it would be possible to pick up additional bodyguards in Denver, regular Pinkerton guards. The Duke had refused. "I do not want my train to look like a military expedition. We will go on as we are."

Raider doubted that Doc would have checked in with the local office anyhow. The two of them had talked about it before splitting up in Cheyenne, and they had both agreed to let that particular pleasure pass on by, each for a different reason. As usual, Raider was woefully behind in his daily reports, and Doc was afraid that somehow this windfall of luxury living he was presently enjoying might somehow get snatched from him if his skinflint employers discovered just how much he was enjoying himself.

Their official reason, however—if they were ever queried—was that the Duke had ordered them to tell no one where he was. Granted, it was a flimsy excuse, but it would do for the time being, so the thing to do was to leave headquarters in blissful ignorance.

Which was all very well, but of course Raider could not use the agency to help in tracking down Doc. However, being a resourceful man, and knowing his partner well, Raider solved this problem by simply checking the city's most expensive and luxurious hotels.

They finally found Doc and the two ducal ladies in the Hotel Metropole, sharing a large three-bedroom suite. The hotel's floor staff tried to stop the Duke and Raider from going upstairs, but wisely desisted after collecting some minor bruises.

When they arrived in front of the suite, the Duke simply opened the door and walked into the living room. The only person there was Sophie. She was half lying, half sitting on a large couch, totally naked, eating an éclair and drinking champagne. When Raider and the Duke walked in she made no move to run for the bedroom or cover herself, but merely took another bite of the éclair, smiled, and said gaily, "Willie! You're back!"

"Obviously," he said dryly. Sophie had by now stood up. Raider quickly turned to leave, but not until he had taken a good long look at all that rosy German flesh, an appreciative appraisal of the long sleek legs, the deep full breasts, the soft curve of stomach.

Sophie stepped into the Duke's arms, pressing her body tightly against his. While she was doing this, she smiled at Raider over the Duke's shoulder. And winked.

The Duke pushed her away. "Go get some clothes on," he snapped.

"Why . . . Willie," she replied, pouting. But there was something in the Duke's expression, a new set to his face that made her obey.

"No . . . you stay," the Duke said to Raider, who was half out the door. So Raider had the pleasure of watching Sophie's incomparable ass sashay through the bedroom doorway until the door closed behind it. He half expected some kind of sunset affect, a final glow after the setting of such radiant beauty. But there was nothing. Merely a closed door.

Then there was the sudden sound of half-stifled, intimate laughter from behind another bedroom door, just to the left of the one Sophie had gone through. Neither the Duke nor Raider had any difficulty recognizing Doc and Emma's voices. For a moment the Duke's eyes held a very dangerous glint. Then he shrugged. "When the cat's away, the mice will play," he muttered. He turned toward Raider, his expression neutral. "That's an old saying we have in Wittgenstein."

"We got the same sayin' here."

Apparently there was some kind of connecting door between the two bedrooms, because they could now hear Sophie's voice, hissing excited warnings to Doc and Emma from within. Doc and Emma immediately fell silent. Two minutes later Doc came out into the suite's living room, flushed, and showing evidence of having dressed very hurriedly. "Raider . . . Your Royal Highness. You've returned."

"How perceptive," the Duke murmured, looking Doc over critically. A moment later Emma came out of Sophie's room, fortifying the impression that there must indeed be connecting doors between the two bedrooms. She too showed signs of having dressed very quickly, and if anything was even more flushed than Doc.

Tension lay heavy in the air until the Duke abruptly said, in a normal tone of voice, "I need a bath."

"Oh . . . yes," Emma said, then pointed to Sophie's door. "In there. That's your room . . . yours and Sophie's."

The Duke looked at her intently, as if silently asking who she shared her room with, then he nodded and walked past his sister on his way toward the bedroom door. She looked back at him rather nervously—until he gave her a huge wink.

Meanwhile, Raider had been staring at his partner in some amazement. "Why you sly ol' dog..." he started to say, until Doc's murderous glare silenced him. Raider then looked away as Emma turned to Doc, sighing in relief, as if to say, "It'll be all right."

And it was. Doc and Emma had, of course, to be very discreet when the Duke was present. Good form alone required that much. But soon the little group had more or less resumed its earlier manner of gay abandon. The women were quite taken by Denver. After all that time out on the plains, they were rediscovering the world of shops, restaurants, and entertainment.

"They have everything here," Sophie gleefully told the Duke. "It's almost like a real city. Why, they even have entertainers who've come all the way from Europe!"

Which was true. There was money in Denver, flowing in from the gold and silver mines in the mountains. Attracted by all that wealth, and by the wild generosity of the miners who daily risked their lives to dig it out of the ground, Europe's parasitical hordes were flocking in, men like Oscar Wilde, the Duke of Cumberland, Italian opera singers, magicians, poets. Wilde was the most popular with the miners, mostly because of the prodigious amounts of raw whiskey he could consume without falling down.

The Duke dutifully squired his sister and his mistress to whatever new entertainment momentarily caught their fancy. But Raider noticed that all the while his eyes kept straying up to the mountains.

Denver is situated on a brushy plain at the foot of truly awesome mountains. The Front Range rises up out of the plain only forty or so miles away, row on row of high, rugged peaks. Mountains dominate the scenery. It's only natural that the eye should rise toward them, but Raider

was sure that at least part of the Duke's interest in those
mountains had something to do with his experiences in the
Dakotas.

One evening, while the four of them were dining at
Charpiot's, feasting on duck, chops, and fish, at the gourmet rate of fifty cents per person, the Duke brought up the
subject of leaving Denver. "Just for a trip," he amended,
noticing the looks of dismay on the ladies' faces. "I would
like to see the Garden of the Gods. We'll go down for a
couple of days. The railroad runs most of the way there,
and after that, carriages are available."

Sophie was captivated by the idea, partly because of the
picturesque name of the place, and partly because it
sounded like an easy and comfortable trip. Doc and Emma
were a little less pleased. They would be pressed more
tightly into the others' company, which would give them
less time for each other.

But go they did. The next day the train crew was
rounded up, most of them looking rather the worse for
wear. One of them did not make it back at all. By the next
morning they were underway.

They made the short trip south to Colorado Springs in a
few hours. They had wired ahead, and a comfortable carriage was waiting for them at the railhead. They set off,
laden down with baskets of cold food, colder wine, and
bottles of cognac. Sophie gabbled cheerfully all along the
way, occasionally casting speculative looks at Raider when
she thought the Duke wasn't watching. By now she,
Emma, and Doc had heard all about Raider and the Duke's
adventures in the north, including the duel with Manteufel.
To Sophie, the violence of it all had added a new luster to
Raider's desirability.

Memories of her and Emma's kidnapping had also left a
lingering residual breathlessness deep down in the pit of
her stomach. The Duke and Raider had not been told about
the kidnapping; Emma and Sophie had made Doc promise
not to mention it. They were afraid that they might be sent

away to some more secure location if the Duke heard that their lives had been in such terrible danger.

They arrived at the Garden of the Gods just before sundown. The eerie beauty of the place drove all other thoughts from the travelers' minds. Huge, strangely shaped rocks thrust upward from out of a thin screen of greenery. The very strangeness of these rock shapes imparted a feeling of reverence and awe.

"I see why they call it the Garden of the Gods," the Duke said, visibly impressed.

They camped out that night, sleeping in the open, or rather, nearly sleeping in the open, because tents and camp cots had been brought along in the carriage, and everyone was able to remain quite clean and comfortable. Only Raider insisted on spreading his bedroll on the hard red earth.

Sophie was fascinated by Raider's bedroll, or soogan, as it was called locally, and she came over to take a closer look. Raider had made the bedroll himself, years before, out of a pair of old overcoats that he'd picked up for a dime in a secondhand store in Laramie. The bedroll had an oilskin covering for when it rained, and was stuffed with old wool for warmth. The smell was awesome, the soogan not having been cleaned since Raider had built it. But it was warm.

Sophie noticed a small scorched hole in the top, about halfway down. "What's that?" she asked.

"Bullet hole."

"Oh . . . somebody shot at you?"

"Uh-uh. The bullet was travelin' in the other direction. Some idiot tried to sneak up on me at night with a knife. Had my gun in there with me. Always do. I got him just before he got me."

"Oh," Sophie said in a small voice, then walked away, glancing back from time to time at the bullet hole.

The Duke had insisted on having a tent of his own. He pitched it about a quarter mile from the tents of the others, up among some of the more spectacular rocks. Raider and Doc at first tried to dissuade him, claiming that he'd be more vulnerable out there on his own. But the Duke insisted. "It is a crime not to be by oneself in a place like this."

After thinking that one over for a moment, Raider nodded in agreement.

Doc looked thoughtfully after the Duke as he walked away to gather his belongings. "What the hell's gotten into him?" he asked.

"The Black Hills," Raider said shortly. Then he too walked away.

Sophie came to Raider's bed a few hours before dawn. The first he knew of it was when he sensed something moving near his bedroll. He slid his hand down to where his Remington lay inside the soogan. The wooden grips were warm against his palm. He lightly rested his thumb on the hammer, turning his head to where he thought the movement was.

He saw a whitish blur that quickly materialized into a totally naked Sophie. She dropped down onto her knees next to Raider's bedroll. "This is a wonderful place to be naked, isn't it?" she whispered.

He looked around at the grotesque shapes of the rock formations. The moon was nearly full. The rocks glowed eerily in its cold light. "Yeah. Guess so."

For a moment he considered sending her back to her tent. But she was right. It was a very special kind of night. Besides, he wanted her. It had been a long time, and now here she was, only an arm's reach away, in all her glorious nakedness, obviously eager to crawl into his soogan. And just like the first time, he found himself unable to turn her down.

Of course, there was no way the both of them could fit into his soogan together; it was a tight enough fit for Raider himself. So they made love on top of the bedroll, with the moon shining its soft tricky lovers' light down onto their intertwined bodies, turning what they were doing into the greatest of mysteries.

Raider sent the girl back to her tent an hour before dawn. He'd noticed that the Duke was becoming an early riser. Yet, as Raider watched Sophie's glorious naked haunches swaying off toward her tent, matching in majesty the surrounding rock formations, he had the peculiar feeling that the Duke really might not care. Raider toyed with the idea that the Duke might even have gone off on his own to set the whole thing up. It was almost as if . . . as if the Duke were somehow getting ready to leave them all, to say goodbye to the whole damned traveling circus.

The morning sun brought well-lighted reality back to the world. The entire camp was up early, including Sophie, looking radiant and quite fulfilled. Doc and Emma, on the other hand, looked decidedly tired. No doubt the night's moonlight magic had had its erotic effect on them too.

The Duke came back to the camp about an hour after sunup, exhibiting quite a decisive air. "You and me," he said to Raider, "we are going to hunt sheep up in the mountains."

CHAPTER SEVENTEEN

Having been a horseman all his adult life, Raider was uncomfortable afoot. Toiling up the nearly sheer slope, he quietly cursed the cramps in his calves. Part of it was the moccasins. He had worn high-heeled boots for so long that his Achilles tendons had shortened. The low heels of the moccasins were painfully stretching them back into shape.

However, despite the cramps, the scenery made it all worthwhile. Mountains, mountains everywhere, stretching off to the horizon in jagged green and blue ridges. The view was best when you got to the top, of course, and they still had a ways to go to get to the top of this particular ridge. The Duke had caught sight of a huge ram up on that ridge, and he was determined to go after it.

He and Raider had been in the mountains for nearly two weeks now. They'd been on foot for the last five days, having left their mounts and the packhorses far below, in the care of the two men they'd brought with them as helpers—helpers that the Duke had eventually decided he did not care to have along. "I want to feel these mountains the way they were meant to be felt," the Duke had said to Raider.

Raider had to admit that the Duke was doing a damned good job of roughing it. They had nothing with them but what they could carry on their backs, which consisted mostly of their weapons and bedrolls. The ground was their bed. They shot or trapped their food.

Raider had to fight down a grin each time he looked at the Duke. His Highness was beginning to resemble an old mountain man from twenty years before. He was wearing a

159

tattered pair of trousers and a buckskin jacket he'd bought from a miner. The battered shapeless wreck on his head could only loosely be called a hat, but it kept off the sun and the moisture. Soft moccasins and a week's growth of beard completed the picture. If the other crowned heads of Europe could only see him now! Yep. The Duke was shaping up. He was turning out to be a lot tougher than Raider had imagined.

The Duke seemed to revel in his present situation. "A man feels so free out here," he told Raider one night over their small campfire. "One has no responsibilities except to stay alive."

Which was more or less the way Raider saw it. Of course, Raider himself had the additional responsibility of not only keeping himself alive but of keeping the Duke alive too. Although responsibility was becoming a poor word to describe what he felt. No. It was friendship now, more than anything else. Raider and the Duke were slowly becoming friends, and you watched a friend's back.

They toiled higher, up a slope so steep that their upper bodies were bent nearly parallel to the ground. They'd had to sling their rifles on their backs so that they could use their hands to grasp hold of bushes and rocks. Raider gritted his teeth at the pain in his calves, but if the Duke could do it, so could he.

"There he is!" the Duke hissed, freezing in place. Raider froze too, looking in the direction the Duke was looking. Yes, there above them, maybe another three hundred yards, was the bighorn ram. "Biggest one I ever saw," Raider whispered.

The ram, apparently not having seen them, or if it had, not considering them a sufficient threat, slowly walked over the other side of a ridge and out of sight.

"Come on," Raider hissed. "Let's get around to where we can see him."

It took them another hour to get into position, but they

finally reached a place where they could stand upright. Raider and the Duke eagerly scanned the landscape, looking for their quarry. Suddenly, there he was, only about two hundred yards away now, outlined very clearly against the skyline.

The big animal was standing on a knifelike ridge that fell off into precipices on either side. It was hard to see how he stood there at all, but stand he did, and regally, head high, massive horns curling down toward his back, legs straight, eyes unafraid.

Unafraid even though Raider was pretty sure the ram knew they were there. His killers. "Go on...shoot," Raider murmured to the Duke.

The Duke slowly slipped his slung rifle off his shoulder. He was carrying the big Sharps that Dull Ax had so contemptuously rejected. He slowly brought the rifle up to his shoulder. The sight was already set for two hundred yards. He laid his cheek against the stock. Now he could see the ram over the sights. He was still standing motionless, although his head had turned slightly toward them.

The Duke knew that the ram was watching him. They'd been spotted. Still, the animal did not run. The Duke looked over the sights again, framing the ram right on top of the front blade. Then he partially lowered the rifle and took a better look. Particularly at the precipices that fell off on either side of the ram. If he killed the ram, it would fall down, down, out of sight. Probably into some place where they would never be able to reach it. He would never be able to recover those magnificent horns; they would never grace the wall of his castle.

Is that all I want to kill that beautiful animal for? the Duke suddenly wondered. For his horns alone? Which will never look as magnificent on a wall as they look on his head?

The Duke pointed the rifle higher, aiming a foot over the ram's head, and squeezed the trigger. The sound of the shot was deafening, echoing and re-echoing from crag to crag. The ram's head jerked higher. For an instant he continued to stare at the Duke, then he jumped, performing a magnificent leap that took him from his ridge top to a rocky platform lower down. A moment later he was gone, vanished.

Raider looked over at the Duke. For a moment their eyes met. Then Raider nodded. The Duke looked away. "Let's go back down," he said.

They had just turned to go when suddenly, without warning, an enormous grizzly burst out of a thick patch of brush about thirty yards away and stood up on its hind legs, facing them. Bear and men stood looking at one another for several seconds. "Don't make any fast moves, Duke. Just keep on movin' downhill," Raider muttered.

They started to move away from the bear, but suddenly it roared very loudly. Raider wondered why—until he saw the cub. It was already half-grown, but still a cub in Momma Bear's eyes. And they were in between the cub and Momma, heading straight toward it.

The grizzly suddenly dropped down on to all fours and charged. "Run, Duke!" Raider shouted, trying to get his rifle off his back, remembering that the Duke had not reloaded after firing at the ram.

Raider got his rifle free, all right, but it was only a Winchester .44-40, too damned light a caliber to run around shooting at grizzlies with. But he fired anyhow, pumping two rounds into the charging animal.

The bullets hurt, and had the effect of temporarily halting the grizzly's charge, but didn't put it down. Bellowing with pain and rage, the huge beast reared up in front of Raider, and before he could fire again, knocked the rifle from his hands with one casual swipe of its massive paw.

Raider jumped back as a second swipe of that paw raked the air in front of his face. His foot caught on a root and he fell flat on his back. Scuttling backward on hands and feet, he did his best to create some distance between himself and the bear, but he knew he didn't stand a chance. The bear was towering over him, roaring, swaying, its little eyes red with rage, its mouth a gaping red hole bordered with unbelievably big gleaming white teeth.

Raider was desperately reaching for his bowie when he heard a thunderous roar from his left. He actually saw the bullet strike the bear's right side, about a foot below the armpit. Dust flew, and the bear reeled to its left.

The Duke had reloaded and fired, and now he was reloading again, his fingers fumbling a little as he flipped open the Sharps's breach, extracting the still-smoking empty shell. A quick reach down toward his cartridge belt to locate another round, but now the bear had seen him. A moment's slow animal cogitation and the bear finally realized where this latest assault had come from.

"Run, Duke!" Raider shouted, leaping to his feet. He charged after the bear, which was now swaying inexorably toward the Duke, still on its hind feet and still roaring bear curses.

The animal towered over the Duke. It was at least eight feet tall. The Duke held his ground, appearing very calm as he finally slipped the big Sharps round into the chamber. *Click* went the action as he locked it. And *click* again as he pulled the hammer back.

He had no time to aim. He shoved the rifle forward, poking it at the bear. The muzzle was only a foot from the animal's chest when the rifle went off. Flame charred the thick fur. The bullet slammed on in, tearing a chunk off the animal's heart. The bear staggered back, roaring, shuddering, its huge arms flailing the air.

Raider was almost on it, raising his bowie high to plunge it into the bear's back, when the mortally wounded animal finally fell, crashing down onto its side. Even so, the Duke repeated the loading ritual, extracting the empty cartridge and inserting another round into the rifle's breach. He'd just had a very powerful lesson about the hazards of an empty rifle.

Raider slipped his bowie back into its sheath and walked rather unsteadily over to the Duke. "Thanks, Duke," he said with great feeling. "I owe you one."

The Duke grinned at him. "And I owe you many."

CHAPTER EIGHTEEN

Momma Bear was dead, but there was still Baby Bear to consider. Or perhaps Junior Bear would be a more accurate appellation, since it was quite a good-sized cub. It stood about forty yards away, whining as it looked over at its fallen mother. Raider contemplated shooting it, since he hated leaving a cub alone without a mother to look after it. But, at the Duke's prodding, he decided that it was probably mature enough to survive on its own, so he ran it off by placing a few rifle shots around its feet.

They then skinned the dead grizzly. "You earned this one," Raider said to the Duke, grinning. "It was a clear case of self-defense."

Packing the hide down the mountain was no easy task. They took turns carrying the heavy, malodorous burden. It was a day later when they finally reached the place where they had left the horses—to find Doc waiting there for them.

"I wanted to get hold of you two before you came back to Denver," Doc explained. "It's von Bock. He's shown up in town, and the scuttlebutt is that he's recruiting a gang of thieves and killers. It's not too hard to guess what for."

"Well, hell, then," Raider replied, "we'll just skip Denver and ride on west."

Doc shook his head. "I thought of that, but it would just be putting off the inevitable, wouldn't it? That made me start thinking about ways to end this thing once and for all."

"Yes. I like that idea," the Duke cut in. "I will meet von Bock face to face and settle this between the two of us."

"I'm certain that would be the most honorable way, Your Highness, if von Bock would meet you on those terms, but I doubt he would. I'm sure that his orders are straightforward and simple—to kill you. He'll go at it in whatever manner works best."

"So what's your idea?" Raider asked.

"Well, I went to see McParland. . . ."

"What? You did what?" Raider demanded, horrified. James McParland was the manager of the Denver western regional office of the Pinkerton National Detective Agency. He was a hard man, and one both Raider and Doc avoided whenever possible.

"It's okay," Doc said soothingly. "Sure, he was a bit upset at first that we hadn't checked in regularly over the past couple of weeks, but I settled all that. And after I told him about von Bock and what he was doing, we also settled on a plan."

Raider's eyebrows rose. "If McParland was in on it, it must be some plan."

"It is. Now here's how it goes. McParland figures that von Bock won't move against the Duke in Denver; he might end up with his head in a noose. And he's found out that the Duke is too well guarded for small-scale attacks, so my guess is that he'll probably use that new gang of his to hit the train way out somewhere where there's nobody else around. He's collected maybe twenty men. That should be enough."

"So?"

"So we bait a trap."

The next half hour was spent arguing over the details of McParland's plan, but the basic idea itself everyone found acceptable. The Duke's one insistence was that he be there when the trap was sprung.

"But Your Highness," Doc protested. "The whole idea is to keep you out of harm's way."

"No. If men are going to risk their lives for me, then I must be there too."

Nothing could shake him on this point, although Doc argued with him all during the long ride back to Denver. Raider, on the other hand, sided with the Duke. "It's his damned life," he said to Doc. "Let him do what he wants with it."

The Duke's single concession was to remove the women from the line of fire. They were sequestered in their hotel suite, much to their disgust, while the train was made ready for departure. Part of the plan was to pretend to leave secretly, but also to make sure that word about the departure leaked out well in advance. That was the cheese for the trap.

On the day of departure, the Duke and his two ladies were seen to board the train. The two ladies were, in reality, two lightly built male Pinkerton agents wearing women's clothing. Flushing red from Raider's jibes about how lovely they looked, the two sat conspicuously near the windows of the railway car, between the Duke and the outside, just in case McParland had been wrong and a sniper attack was planned before the train left the yard. The agents were to provide a human bullet screen.

"Looks like you're gonna be cannon fodder, ladies," Raider snickered evilly.

The train got under way a few minutes later. When it was well away from the yard, and thus out of sight of whomever might have been watching it—and Raider was certain that von Bock would have had men there to report on anything unusual—he went into the car that he and Doc normally shared. "Okay boys," he cut out, "come on in, but keep low."

Ten heavily armed Pinkerton agents looked up from where they had been hiding. They had slipped aboard late the night before. "Hey, pretty fancy way you been livin', Raider," one of them snickered. "Bet you're even wearin' silk underwear."

"Get movin', Johnson," Raider shot back. "Or you'll be wearin' my boot up your ass."

The men half crawled into the Duke's car, keeping below window level, and posted themselves on the floor, where they would be invisible from the outside. "When do you think they're gonna hit us?" Johnson asked Raider.

"Somewhere between here and California."

"Great. Glad to hear that," Johnson grumbled. "Nothin' like hunkerin' down on a cold hard floor to help the time pass by. Say, anybody got any cards?"

"No cards. Keep alert."

"Ah. . . ."

The train steamed along slowly. More slowly than usual, but that was part of the plan too. It chugged out of Denver and headed north, back toward Cheyenne and the main line west.

And nothing happened. The entire distance to Cheyenne was trouble-free. Nothing happened in Cheyenne either, and it was smooth sailing out the other side of the little town, as they headed west toward Utah.

Raider was beginning to grow a little worried. He'd had to shove the extra men back into their cramped quarters when the train was passing through Cheyenne, so they wouldn't be seen. They were growing tired now, and bored. The big danger was that they would grow careless.

"I don't like this," Doc said. "Maybe we planned wrong."

Raider shook his head. "No, I don't think so. There wasn't much chance of 'em hittin' us out in the Colorado flats, anyhow. We'd o' been able to see 'em comin' from too far away. It's when we get to the mountains that we gotta keep our eyes peeled."

It was nearly dark when they reached the first foothills of the Rockies. "Get the engineer in here," Raider said to Doc. "I gotta talk to him."

Five minutes later the engineer came banty-walking into the car. "What's on your mind this time?" he asked sarcastically. "Plannin' a rest stop?"

"Maybe, maybe not. Right now I want to know about

train schedules. For instance, are any other trains scheduled to come through here about this time?"

Scrunching up his beady little eyes in concentration, the engineer consulted his schedules. "Nope. Not till a little after ten o'clock. There'll be nothin' much movin' before that."

"Then it's probably gonna happen pretty soon. Check me out on this. We're gonna be headin' uphill in a little while, slowin' down, ain't that right?"

"Yep."

"No other traffic in sight."

"Nope."

"So can you think of a better time to hit us?"

"Nope."

"Good. Then get back to your engine. Don't be no hero, now. If you gotta stop the train, stop it."

"Yep."

The rest of the men quickly picked up Raider's mood of anticipation. They filed back into the car and spread themselves out, rifles ready. The train was visibly slowing now as the grade increased. They were starting the long climb up toward the Continental Divide.

Doc got up from where he'd been sitting and came over to Raider. "I hope they didn't get held up in Cheyenne," he said worriedly.

"They probably did . . . a little. Just to make it look like they wasn't followin' us. That means we'll have to hold von Bock off a little longer, that's all."

"Yeah. If we can," Doc muttered gloomily.

The attack came a bare five minutes later. The train was well into the mountains now, moving quite slowly. The rails ran through a deepening gorge, which meant there was a lot of high ground quite close by, overlooking the train.

"This is a real good place for it," Raider murmured to Doc.

Suddenly he was almost knocked off his feet by a tremendous jerk as the engineer applied the brakes. A pile of logs was lying across the tracks about a hundred yards ahead. The train slid to a shuddering halt, the steel wheels screaming against the rails. Then all of a sudden most of the windows on the right-hand side of the car blew inwards under a hail of gunfire.

"This is it!" Raider shouted, snatching up his rifle and thrusting it out one of the shattered windows.

Others were doing the same. However, the man dressed in Sophie's clothes had been hit, and was lying half out of his seat, cursing, one hand pressed to his bleeding shoulder. Other men were following Raider's example, crouching low in the seats, ready to fire out through the windows.

"Here they come!" somebody shouted.

A dozen men were running downslope through the pines, firing at the train as they came on. Others gave them covering fire from back in the trees. All the attackers had been told that they would have an easy time of it, that there were only a few men on the train, and that most of them were either servants or train crew. Imagine their surprise, then, when the train windows erupted in flashes of flame from at least a dozen gun muzzles, and a hail of lead flew their way.

Three went down immediately. The rest quickly took cover behind tree trunks or rocks. Angered, they dug in deep and began blasting away at the train, especially at the car where all the firing was coming from.

That might eventually have won them the day. They had mobility, and the train's defenders were trapped inside. Plus it was already dusk, and rapidly growing darker. In a little while it would be dark enough for one of them to crawl close enough to lob a stick of dynamite under the car and blow it apart. They had been provided with plenty of dynamite.

Life was hectic inside the Duke's car. All the windows

on one side had been shot out by now, and it was only a matter of time until some of the attackers moved around to the other side. Another man had been hit, this one much more seriously than the first. Bloody foam bubbled up out of a hole in his chest. He'd been hit in the lungs.

Raider crawled along the floor, encouraging the defenders. Broken glass crunched under his knees. "Damn it, Duke!" he shouted. "Get your fuckin' head outta that window!"

"That's the only way that I can see to shoot!" the Duke protested angrily.

"You're gonna be seein' things through an extra eye if you stick your head up that way. Hunker down next to the seat. Make a smaller target outta yourself."

The Duke complied, grumbling, however, that he'd be lucky to hit anything this way. Raider left him alone. He had other things to worry about. Like staying alive. His men had fired back too soon, giving the attackers a chance to find cover. He'd hoped to catch them out in the open, in the middle of their charge, and mow them down.

The terrain didn't help; the slopes and the trees were too damned close. He was also worried about dynamite. He recognized the damage that a well-placed charge could inflict on the car. "You an' you," he ordered two men. "Get on up to the coal tender. Look down the sides of the train. Shoot anybody that gets close."

The two men raced away. He detailed two more to guard the sides of the train from the caboose. That left him with damned few men in the Duke's car. There was now so much firing coming from outside that most of his men had to crouch very low, which hindered their ability to fire back. It was growing damned dark, too. Another ten minutes of this and the attackers might be able to successfully rush the train.

And then he heard it, very close, not more than a few hundred yards behind the caboose, the heavy chuffing of a laboring locomotive. He might have heard it sooner, and so might the attackers, if the sound of gunfire had not been so loud.

Raider rushed back to the caboose. His two men were still inside, guarding the track. "Goddamn it, here they come at last!" one yelled gleefully, pointing back down the track.

There it was indeed—a short train made up of two coaches and several boxcars. It came to a hasty shuddering stop about two hundred yards behind the Duke's train. A moment later men began pouring out of the coaches, running toward a screen of trees downslope from where the attackers were dug in, thus flanking them.

Raider ran back to the Duke's car. "Don't get careless now, boys," he shouted. "Keep pouring lead outta those windows!"

Fifty men had arrived on that second train, all armed to the teeth. They quickly made an end run around the attackers, who were already so well pinned down by the increased fire from the train that they could not easily slip away into the trees. Now they were being hit from both the front and the flank. They began to panic. Many leaped up to run, but were cut down almost at once. Those who remained to fight survived a while longer, but they had little real chance.

Still, the shooting continued for another ten minutes. The growing darkness delayed the end, giving cover to the attackers, who had now become the hunted. Raider had left the car and was directing the fight, helping blast a last few stubborn men out of hiding. Finally, the few survivors had the brains to surrender. They came in out of the trees, hands over their heads, most of them bleeding from wounds.

Raider sought out the leader of the men from the relief train. "Round 'em up," he said, pointing to the captives. "And keep your eye out for a German bastard with a big mustache and a scar on his face."

"What do I do with him when I find him?"

"Well, I'd kinda like to hear that he got killed in the fightin'."

"Yeah. Can do."

"Okay. We're on our way."

After his wounded had been taken off and put into the second train, Raider reboarded the Duke's train. The Duke, his face smudged with gunsmoke, walked up to him. "Von Bock?" he asked.

"They haven't found him yet."

The Duke nodded. "I would have liked to have talked to him one last time."

"I figure he's probably dead."

The Duke raised his head sharply, looking at Raider questioningly.

"My feelin' is that he got killed in the fightin'. There was one hell of a lot o' lead flyin' around out there."

The Duke slowly nodded. "It all makes me very sad," he said in a low voice. "This is not the kind of hunting I had in mind when I first decided to come to your country."

CHAPTER NINETEEN

It was anything but a luxury train that pulled into the train-yards at Ogden late the next day. The woodwork on the coaches was splintered, the metal was pocked with bullet holes, and almost all the glass had been shot out of the windows.

With the Duke's vast monetary resources, it was not too difficult to order some more cars. It would be a few days, however, before the new train could be assembled and moved out to Ogden.

Raider, Doc, and the Duke stayed in an Ogden hotel as bachelors until Sophie and Emma joined them on the second day. A Pinkerton operative accompanied the women, obviously having enjoyed the work. With one last appreciative glance at Sophie, who was disappearing into the Duke's bedroom, smiling back at him over her shoulder, the operative buttonholed Raider and Doc. "That German you were looking for. Von Bock. We couldn't find his body. Some of the survivors say they saw him hightailing it into the woods near the end of the fight."

"Damn!" Raider swore under his breath. "That bastard has more lives than a cat. Now we gotta start worryin' about him all over again."

"Well, maybe not so much," the operative said. "He was on foot in the middle of the Rockies, maybe hurt, and after that shoot-out, probably kinda just a little bit discouraged."

"I'm afraid that nothing short of death would discourage von Bock," Doc said gloomily.

They decided not to tell the Duke. He appeared to have enough weight on his shoulders as it was. He now seemed to want to get the trip over with as quickly as possible. As soon as the new train was ready he asked Raider and Doc to get everyone aboard. "We will go straight on to San Francisco," he said. "From there, Sophie, Emma, and myself will board a steamship for the Orient."

The trip west was quite a gloomy one. Raider was tired of the train and wished he were on a horse again. He was also a little lonely. Since the fight, Sophie had been sticking close to the Duke, with no time to spare for Raider. Doc was in a blue funk now that he knew Emma would be parted from him so soon. He could see no way to get aboard that Orient-bound ship, and even if he could, he knew that it would get him nowhere; it was all nothing but a pipe dream. He and Emma had met, joined, and now would be separated.

The Duke was very quiet all during the trip west, sitting silently for hours at a time, watching the matchless western scenery move by outside the train's windows. Their route took them down the western slopes of the Rockies, past Great Salt Lake, and down into the desert. The desert fascinated the travelers. Hour after hour they watched its bleak severeness pass by. On the second afternoon the women prevailed on the Duke to have the train stopped. They got down for about an hour, walking about over the desert floor, marveling at the dryness of the hot, unceasing wind.

They continued on over the Nevada Sink, a huge arid depression between the Rockies and the Sierra Nevada. It was quite a relief when the train finally began to climb the steep eastern slope of the Sierras. Higher and higher they went, past ridges and through tunnels where dozens of men had died during the laying of the track.

The Duke's mood had improved considerably by the time they were descending the western slopes of those lovely mountains. The vastness of California's great Central Valley spread out below them. Agriculturally, it was an exceptionally rich area. Fields of grain and vegetables stretched away for as far as the eye could see.

"What incredible wealth," the Duke murmured.

They left the train at Sacramento. There was a certain poignancy to the leave-taking; the train had been the center of their lives for some time now. Adventures had unfolded around and inside those luxurious railroad cars. Only Raider was genuinely glad to see the last of them.

They rode a commercial train to the eastern shores of San Francisco Bay, then crossed the bay on a ferryboat, with most of the deck space taken up by their baggage. The Duke's party had accumulated many additional possessions during the trip, to add to the mountain of trunks and boxes that they had brought with them from Europe. All of it was to be taken back to Wittgenstein.

San Francisco was the greatest success of the entire journey. The women were delighted with the civilized nature of that lovely little city by the bay. They exclaimed over the fine shops and the musical shows and other entertainments. They were favorably impressed by the huge houses of the silver barons, whose money flowed in thick shiny streams from the Nevada mines.

The Duke was particularly enthusiastic about the proliferation of fine restaurants. Most of the world's better cuisine was abundantly available. He and Doc spent days wandering from restaurant to restaurant, growing visibly fatter.

They were headquartered in the magnificent new Palace Hotel, which had opened the previous year. Seven stories high, with eight hundred rooms, it was the finest hotel in the western part of North America. A great arched entranceway led into the hotel's Grand Court, an enormous area of marble masonry. The Duke's party inhabited two huge suites, with the Duke and Sophie in one, Raider and Doc in the other. Emma's whereabouts were somewhat fluid, depending on when she could sneak over to Doc's huge bedroom and still maintain at least some show of noble propriety.

The Duke fell in love with the cable cars. There was, as yet, only one line, running up Clay Street, from Kearney to the top of the hill. He rode the cars often, mostly for the view, which was, as always, magnificent. The blue of the bay swept north and south, with the dun Berkeley Hills spreading low on the far side. The fog which regularly crept in through the Golden Gate was startlingly white in the sunshine.

Chinatown was a big attraction for the Duke and the ladies. Raider usually went with them when they walked its narrow streets. "We won't need to take that boat," the Duke joked. "See?" he said, pointing to a party of pigtailed Chinese, who were dressed in long cotton jackets topped off by conical straw hats. "We're already in the Orient."

There was a darker side to Chinatown. The white citizens, jealous of the industriousness of the Chinese, and hurting from current high unemployment, did everything they could to rid the city of them. Discriminatory laws were passed, which made it very difficult for the Chinese to earn a living. Sometimes mob violence flared, which was the main reason Raider went along with the Duke and the ladies.

On some of the nicer afternoons, they all went to the new Golden Gate Park, formerly a wasteland of bare sand dunes, which was now being planted with grass and thousands of trees. For a while it seemed as if the ducal party would remain in San Francisco forever. But after three weeks, the Duke showed signs of wanting to move on. Doc swallowed the lump in his throat as he thought about being parted form Emma. He was honest enough to admit to himself, however, that his feet were beginning to grow just the least little bit itchy. Having known all along that a parting would eventually be necessary, he was emotionally prepared.

And then a ghost from the past suddenly intruded into this relaxed idyll. One afternoon, the Duke, Doc, Raider, and the ladies were crossing a side lobby of the hotel, walking toward the elevators that would take them up to their floor. They had all been out together for a sumptuous meal at the Poulet d'Or, the city's finest French restaurant. Relaxed and replete, they had nearly made it to the elevators when a figure suddenly stepped out from behind a potted palm.

Von Bock.

Raider and Doc were on him before he had completed a full step toward the Duke. Von Bock's right hand was hidden in his right coat pocket, starting to pull something out into the open. Raider pinned von Bock's arm to his side; he could feel the hardness of the pistol inside the pocket.

Doc had his little .32 out and was pointing it at von Bock's head, but the Duke stepped in and took hold of his arm. "No. Put it away. I don't think he can really do much harm to any of us. Just look at him."

Von Bock was indeed not looking his usual well-groomed and confident self. His clothing was ragged and dirty, his face gaunt and shadowed, his eyes sunken, and he had a dirty rag bound around his neck, through which a slight stain of old blood showed. "Bring him up to the suite," the Duke ordered, turning around and walking calmly toward the elevator.

Raider slid his hand into von Bock's pocket and removed the pistol. Then, with Doc on one side and himself on the other, they hustled von Bock toward the elevator. He put up no resistance at all, but let them lead him as if he were a tired sheep.

The Duke and the two women had already gone up in the elevator, so the two Pinkertons and their captive had to wait for the elevator to descend again. When the doors opened, the operator's eyes swept disapprovingly over von Bock's disheveled appearance. This was clearly not the kind of person the Palace Hotel welcomed. But, with

Raider's hard black eyes boring into his beady little ones, the elevator flunky quickly recognized the wisdom of keeping his own counsel.

The Duke was waiting in the living room of his suite when the two Pinkertons brought von Bock inside. Emma and Sophie were nowhere in sight. "Well, Count," the Duke said quietly. "You don't give up easily, do you?"

"No, I do not," von Bock replied steadily. Raider's arm tightened on the man's arm. He may have looked in bad shape, but the steel in his voice suggested that he was still a dangerous adversary.

Von Bock haughtily shook off Raider's grip. "I have no more weapons with which to fight you," he said icily, turning to look first at Raider, then at the Duke. "You have stopped me at every turn."

"Which is only just," the Duke replied. "You have been engaged in a dishonorable mission."

"Honor? What do you know of honor?" Von Bock burst out bitterly. "You? A man who hides behind an army of cheap mercenaries?"

The Duke smiled. "I assure you, Count, that the Pinkerton Agency is anything but cheap. And these men have become my friends."

Then his smile faded and he became more serious. "However, there is some justice in what you say. I have indeed hidden behind others, let others take risks for me. It doesn't matter that they've been paid to do that; I like to think that in the past I've always had the courage to face my own problems. It is simply that this political mess between myself and Bismarck seems to have addled my judgment. Nothing is quite as it used to be."

"Prince von Bismarck is a great man," von Bock flared. "A great man doing great work."

"Yes, you really believe that, don't you? You believe it so deeply that I suppose you will never stop trying to remove me as long as I continue to oppose Bismarck."

"Never. I will never stop until I have fulfilled my orders."

The Duke sighed. "I suspect that this kind of thinking, Prussian thinking, will cause the world a great deal of future grief. But, the question is, what can be done about it in our present situation?"

"Nothing. Prussia will triumph. The German Reich will be reborn."

"Perhaps, perhaps not. I shudder to think that it might actually happen. Well, I suppose it will. But as for the situation between you and me, von Bock, I suspect that there is only one answer. Your kind of fanaticism must be met head on. Personally."

Suspecting in which direction the conversation was leading, Doc suddenly interrupted. "Your Highness, don't—"

von Bock smiled sardonically. "Listen. The dogs begin to yap."

"That's enough, von Bock," the Duke said sharply. Then, when Doc tried to speak again, he added, "That will be enough from you too, Dr. Weatherbee. From now on this is my affair, and my affair alone."

The Duke turned back to von Bock. "Will sabers be satisfactory to you, Count?"

A mixture of amazement and triumph lit up the Count's tired features. "Of course!"

"Your Highness! No!" Doc burst out.

"Goddamn it, Doc, shut up," Raider said gently.

The Duke walked closer to von Bock, until he was standing directly in front of him. "In two days, then. When you've had a chance to rest."

Over the next twenty-four hours, the ducal suite took on the air of a funeral parlor. Sophie moped, Emma had trouble hiding the fact that her eyes were red, and Doc prowled about nervously. Only Raider and the Duke seemed at all relaxed. In fact, the Duke appeared to be in better humor than during the entire preceding several weeks. His eyes were clear, his step firm, his face relaxed.

"He's found his answer," Raider said to Doc.

"He's probably only found his death," Doc replied wearily.

Raider shrugged. "Sometimes it's the same thing. Facing it is, anyhow. Maybe I can teach him one o' those old Sioux death songs."

"I'm certain that would really encourage him."

"You might be surprised."

The site for the final showdown between Count Otto von Bock, and Wilhelm, Grand Duke of Wittgenstein, was to be about eighty miles south of the city, near a little town called Soquel. Dueling anywhere near the city was liable to attract negative official interest. So, on the afternoon of the second day, the entire party, now augmented by von Bock's presence, took a short-haul train south, toward Camp Capitola and Soquel.

It was a lovely trip. Most of it was along a stretch of rather arid but otherwise beautiful coastline. Mountains stretched inland, sometimes coming to within a few hundred yards of the coast. Heavy lumbering had already destroyed most of the magnificent redwoods that had previously clothed the mountain slopes, but scattered groves still remained.

They arrived at Camp Capitola just as the light was fading. The camp was actually a collection of tents and shanties which were used as holiday accommodations by vacationers from the city. Other accommodations were few, but the Duke's vast purse had provided them with one night's use of a substantial farmhouse.

Everyone gathered in the farmhouse's kitchen, including von Bock. The sea was not very far away, and the sound of the surf was clearly audible. "I find that sound very soothing," the Duke said.

Von Bock nodded at him. "You have more courage than I suspected, Wittgenstein."

The Duke smiled. "And tomorrow you might also discover that I have more skill with a sword than you suspected."

It cannot be said that the farmhouse was a scene of unrestrained jollity that night, although the Duke insisted that they all share a bottle of champagne before going to bed. Raider joined in, but made a face as he tasted the wine. "Too strong for you, gunman?" Von Bock jeered, but with a certain amount of good nature.

Raider looked over at him as he poured a slug of whiskey into his champagne. "If there's anythin' left of you after tomorrow morning, I get seconds, big-mouth."

"Agreed."

The next morning, everyone was awake before first light. A carriage had been hired, large enough for them all, and while it was still dark, but with a faint lightening in the eastern sky, they set out together for the location where the duel was to take place.

It was a small clearing in the midst of a grove of immense redwoods. By the time they arrived, it was fully light, although the light was still somewhat milky—which is one of the reasons duels are fought in the early morning. No dueler wants sunlight in his eyes at a critical moment.

The principals chose their weapons. The Duke had provided a beautiful pair of silver-hilted sabers. The blades were partially blued, with the bluing forming a striking pattern against the brilliance of the unblued parts. The women had been invited to go back to the carriage and wait, but both Emma and Sophie refused. Doc and Raider walked off to the side. Doc was to be the surgeon, although he had protested that in reality he was merely an apothecary. Lacking anyone else, he would have to do.

Von Bock and the Duke strode out onto the soft springy ground. There was no grass, of course; grass does not grow underneath redwoods. Very little does. The first shafts of sunlight were now touching the tops of the immense trees, gilding their dark green feathery needles. With the massive shafts of the trunks rising up on every side, it was as if they were all standing in a vast outdoor cathedral.

The Duke turned to face Raider. He smiled. "As your Indian friends would say, it is a beautiful day to die."

"Or live."

The Duke and the Count faced one another. They raised their swords in the traditional salute. Then both men assumed the on-guard position. The duel had now begun.

Over the next several minutes, Raider was able to recognize how clumsy and amateurish the fight between himself and Manteufel had been. Both von Bock and the Duke were master swordsmen. Moving lightly, their bodies in perfect balance, they advanced and retreated, feinted and thrust, cut and parried, and otherwise did their best to take one another's lives.

At first it was von Bock who seemed to have the edge. He steadily pushed the Duke back, slicing and cutting, aiming principally at his opponent's wrist and head. The Duke acquitted himself well enough, but he was clearly on the defensive.

About two minutes into the fight, von Bock launched a blistering attack. Steel rang against steel. A fleck of blood suddenly appeared on the Duke's right forearm. Emma gasped and took a step forward, but Doc held her back. He himself was less worried; he saw that it was merely a scratch.

von Bock's big offensive had by now somewhat overextended his strength; the past few weeks had been very trying for him, both physically and mentally. He was forced to slow his attack, and he was panting.

This was the time for the Duke to switch over to the attack, and he did so, lunging in again and again, beating at von Bock's blade, tiring his arm. Von Bock fell back, and now it was his turn to be on the defensive.

The fight continued. Von Bock was gasping audibly now. He knew that he was tiring faster than the Duke; his only chance would be to launch one last desperate attack that would end with either himself or the Duke on the ground.

The Duke was somewhat taken by surprise by this final flurry of flashing steel. He missed a step, and the Count's blade slipped past his. The razor-sharp edge of the last few inches below the tip sliced into his left cheek, cutting deep. Blood spurted, and the Duke reeled back.

"Hah! Now!" Von Bock shouted, lunging in again, going for the kill.

But the Duke slipped the Count's blade to the side, and, riposting with a straight lunge, ran his saber right through the center of the Count's chest.

Von Bock shuddered, then stood rock-still. He looked down, staring dumbly at the bright steel embedded in his breast. When the Duke withdrew his blade, von Bock uttered a terrible groan, stood for another second, then fell full-length onto the ground.

Doc was at his side in an instant. von Bock rolled half onto his side and looked up at him. He tried to speak, failed once, then tried again. "Tell Wittgenstein . . . tell him that . . ."

A fountain of blood gushed from his mouth, choking off the words. von Bock's eyes opened wide in agony, then went blank. He was dead.

The Duke, still holding his bloody sword, walked over to where his fallen enemy lay. "The fool," he said, in so low a voice that Doc barely heard him. "He devoted his life to death. And now death is all that he has."

Sophie and Emma came running over. Emma avoided looking down at von Bock. Sophie looked with frank curiosity. "Your face!" Emma cried out, pressing a handkerchief to the deep cut on the Duke's left cheek. "No . . . no. It's nothing," the Duke protested. "I've always wanted a dueling scar. My subjects will love me all the more for it."

Raider prodded von Bock's body with his toe. "Well, Duke, you took care of it yourself, just like you said you would, and now the whole goddamned mess is over."

The Duke looked at him with some surprise. "Over?" he asked. "No, it is not over. How can it be?"

He then looked down at von Bock. "Others will be sent. They will always send them. But for the time being . . . I'm hungry."

Raider grinned. "I heard about a place not far from here, run by some Germans. They got sauerkraut."

The Duke smiled back at him. "Sauerkraut will do just fine."

J.D. HARDIN

"THE MOST EXCITING
WESTERN WRITER SINCE
LOUIS L'AMOUR"
—JAKE LOGAN

___ 06412-3	BOUNTY HUNTER #31	$2.50
___ 07700-4	CARNIVAL OF DEATH #33	$2.50
___ 08013-7	THE WYOMING SPECIAL #35	$2.50
___ 07257-6	SAN JUAN SHOOTOUT #37	$2.50
___ 07259-2	THE PECOS DOLLARS #38	$2.50
___ 07114-6	THE VENGEANCE VALLEY #39	$2.75
___ 07386-6	COLORADO SILVER QUEEN #44	$2.50
___ 07790-X	THE BUFFALO SOLDIER #45	$2.50
___ 07785-3	THE GREAT JEWEL ROBBERY #46	$2.50
___ 07789-6	THE COCHISE COUNTY WAR #47	$2.50
___ 07974-0	THE COLORADO STING #50	$2.50
___ 08032-3	HELL'S BELLE #51	$2.50
___ 08088-9	THE CATTLETOWN WAR #52	$2.50
___ 08669-0	THE TINCUP RAILROAD WAR #55	$2.50
___ 07969-4	CARSON CITY COLT #56	$2.50
___ 08743-3	THE LONGEST MANHUNT #59	$2.50
___ 08774-3	THE NORTHLAND MARAUDERS #60	$2.50
___ 08792-1	BLOOD IN THE BIG HATCHETS #61	$2.50
___ 09089-2	THE GENTLEMAN BRAWLER #62	$2.50
___ 09112-0	MURDER ON THE RAILS #63	$2.50
___ 09300-X	IRON TRAIL TO DEATH #64	$2.50
___ 09343-3	THE ALAMO TREASURE #66	$2.50
___ 09396-4	BREWER'S WAR #67	$2.50
___ 09480-4	THE SWINDLER'S TRAIL #68	$2.50
___ 09568-1	THE BLACK HILLS SHOWDOWN #69	$2.50
___ 09648-3	SAVAGE REVENGE #70	$2.50
___ 09714-5	TRAIN RIDE TO HELL #71	$2.50